# PRINCE
# OF HEARTS

Kiru Taye

First Published in Great Britain in 2020 by
LOVE AFRICA PRESS
103 Reaver House, 12 East Street, Epsom KT17 1HX
www.loveafricapress.com

Available in ebook and paperback

# YADILI SERIES

Prince of Hearts
Killer of Kings
Bad Santa
Rough Diamond
Tough Alliance

Kiru Taye

# PRINCE OF HEARTS

Dear reader,

I love writing stories about characters who challenge perceptions and defy the odds. Duke and Carla are two such people. They do not fit into the regular moulds that society designates. Yet they laugh, cry, hurt, fall in love and hope for a happy future, just like the rest of us.

I hope you enjoy reading their story as much as I loved writing it.

# BLURB

Duke's life is about honour, loyalty, and respect for the business. Nothing else. Yet, one look at Carla across a crowded nightclub, and he breaks his own rules. One night with the seductive woman who calls to him like no other, and he wants to keep her.

But his troubled angel is a mafia princess who lives dangerously on the edge. She plays a desperate prank and sparks a cartel war.

Now, Duke is in a high-stakes battle to keep everything he loves. And he intends to win, come Hell or high water.

Content Warning: contains depictions of drug use and depictions of torture.

# ONE

DUKE ODILI needed a good fuck.

His best friend, Mason or 'Mace' as he was known to close friends, had said words to that effect a week ago—the exact statement being, "Seriously, man. You need to get laid."

Duke hadn't argued. Not that he encouraged anyone to keep a tab on his sexual activities.

However, facts were facts.

A man ruled by duty and discipline, Duke was not given to excessive indulgences.

He'd had to think hard about the last time he'd savoured the soft curves of a woman. Had only worked it out because he'd kept the shitty breakup message from his ex-girlfriend, and he'd read the timestamp—eight months and twenty-five days.

Nine long months of nothing but porn, lube and his hand to achieve sexual gratification.

He was overdue for a weekend devoted to pleasure with a willing partner.

Standing on the balcony of his hotel suite, a briny sea breeze whipped the humid air, cooling his clammy skin.

The crashing of the waves against the sandy shore provided a soundtrack, and the bright moon made it easy to view from the vantage point of ten floors up.

A road separated the beach from the buildings. Bright streetlamps lit the promenade, and only a handful of people strolled past.

The hotel stood on one of the most expensive strips of land along the coastline of western Africa.

Idunnu was an exclusive adult-only resort that catered for the rich and famous. The place presented an 18-hole golf course for anyone so inclined and an entertainment schedule that included live performance acts.

Duke flipped the black plexiglass card in his hand and ran his thumb over the embossed stylised silver logo of Club Arufin, a venue reputed for hedonistic parties.

The concierge had delivered the VIP Pass earlier, and it had cost a small fortune. The name fit the club, a venue for outcasts and outlaws where anything was permissible, and taboos were the norm.

Tonight, Duke needed uninhibited, anonymous sex.

He could visit similar locations in and around his home city. The Odili-owned Opal Casino and Hotel chain also included trendy nightclubs.

However, as a celebrity in his home region, Duke couldn't indulge in anonymous encounters. The women he met knew him on sight and always wanted more than he could give. Hence, his ex-girlfriend accused him of being emotionally unavailable in her last message.

A fair indictment.

He wasn't long-term boyfriend material.

His family and business commitments meant he worked long days and even longer nights. Not that there weren't opportunities to party. Just that he lacked the inclination.

Duke was damaged goods. He'd long accepted that reality. He wouldn't waste anyone's time by promising a future he couldn't deliver.

The trauma of his parents' death haunted him.

Remembering his mother, his chest tightened. Mama sitting in a chair by the bed, reading stories from a book, singing songs in a beautifully lyrical voice, or whispering comforting words when he lay unwell. Brown hair with tight curls twisted into plaits and hazel brown eyes, she'd also had the loveliest smile ever and lit up his life daily with brilliance.

Awash with regret, he scrubbed a hand over his face. He had no mementoes to remember her by except memories. After twenty-four years, those were fading.

Haunted by the hellish memory, he'd employed a private detective to investigate his parents' deaths. So many years had passed, and getting information was slow and tedious.

But sources indicated the answers to his inquiry lay in Lori Osa, the bustling megacity an hour's drive from his current location, partly the reason he'd come here.

He returned indoors and shut the balcony door, locking it. He flicked the wall switch. Diffused yellow light filled the living room. He grabbed the cell phone from the table and pressed the shortcut button.

"Boss," a sleepy male voice replied after a few seconds.

"Jide, we're going out. Have the car ready in thirty minutes." He suppressed the twinge of guilt for waking the young man.

As one of his well-trusted personal security, Jide always had to be ready to move at a moment's notice. An apprentice, he would work his way from the bottom upwards, earning his stripes through the ranks. Maybe one day, he would attain Duke's position if he won it by serving his boss well and showing loyalty to the family.

Duke would have preferred a break from an entourage. But like his designer suits, having an escort twenty-four-seven was a part of his life.

"Sure," Jide replied before cutting off the connection.

A quick shower first, then Duke shaved and dressed. A glance at the full-length mirror showed a tall man in a tailored, two-piece ash silk suit, white shirt, and leather brogues. The colour of the outfit set off his russet skin tone.

Aware of the attraction his looks held for others, he entertained no conceit about it. Apart from the expensive clothes, he hadn't earned his chiselled features. Genetics—something handed down by his parents. If any pride was to be held, it should be for the people who'd made him.

He opened a drawer to pull out a tie but changed his mind and closed it. Image mattered in business, and he wore one on most days. However, there'd be no working for the next few hours. He could live without the tie...and undid the hidden top two buttons of the shirt. Better.

The door to the adjacent room slammed, and footsteps rushed down the hallway.

He glanced at his gold wristwatch and smiled. He didn't abide tardiness, and the men understood this. Jide would be downstairs with the car ready in time. Another reason Duke had selected him for this trip.

He rolled his shoulders as the tightness in his chest loosened.

Time to forget his past and business and focus on the night ahead.

Time to make like the tourist he was supposed to be and get some action.

Handgun locked in the safe, he left the suite and took the elevator to the ground floor.

"Have a good evening, Mr Odili," the uniformed doorman greeted as he held the door to the flashy high-end SUV.

"Thank you," Duke replied, stepping in and relaxing into the soft, tortilla-brown leather.

"Where to, Boss?" Jide asked from the driver's seat as the engine purred to life. The younger man practically lived in denim and t-shirts, so Duke smiled at seeing him in a slate-blue dress shirt and wine-coloured Chinos.

"Arufin."

Jide nodded and eased the car from the spot, heading down the tree-lined avenue out of the walled complex. The extra security ensured the resort remained exclusive, unlike others that had been occasionally overrun by vagrants.

They drove past quiet and gated residential communities characterised by designer malls, coffee shops, and eateries. The middle to upper-class homes lay walled off with private firms providing security, businesses run by the cartels, mostly.

Who better to pay to keep properties safe than the people who would rob them?

Extortion, some said. But even those people didn't trust the police to keep them safe.

Duke figured it was better to keep those boys gainfully employed than to have them idle and broke.

At this hour, there weren't many people—cars or pedestrians—on the roads. When he'd been a boy, a curfew had existed, and no one had been allowed on the streets without prior permission from 9pm until 5am. The restrictions had since been lifted, although most decent people stayed at home past ten o'clock at night.

Of course, decent wasn't a word he'd use to describe himself. The smart, expensive clothes usually fooled people into thinking he was one of the nice ones. All an illusion. He'd learned a long time ago that image was everything.

Thirty minutes later, they arrived in Lori Osa City and drove past the business district with its skyscrapers, into a concrete jungle. Four police officers stood beneath the harsh floodlight at the security checkpoint.

"Stay alert," Duke instructed, reaching for the secured case under the front seat and unclasping the lock.

Inside it sat an Uzi submachine gun as well as hand grenades. Most of their cars had similar equipment for emergencies. Assassinations had been known to occur at checkpoints. One couldn't be too careful, although he hoped they wouldn't need the hidden weapons.

"Yes, Boss," Jide replied as he stepped off the accelerator.

Two of the officers approached, one on each side of the car. The female on Jide's side tapped the window. Her dark uniform showed off her full-bodied curves.

He depressed the button, rolling it down halfway. "Good evening, Officer. How can I help you?"

"It's just a routine stop," she explained and tipped her head to investigate the back seat.

She had a pretty face and a body to match. On a good day, Duke might have smiled and even offered a tip.

But it was late, and he was away from his turf with only Jide as a backup, a risk. In a bid for incognito, he'd chosen only one travelling companion, and it had worked so far. He couldn't afford to prolong the interaction. Her pretty face could be used as a weapon of distraction while others get into positions to attack.

Duke met her gaze with a piercing one, which usually unsettled some people.

She swallowed and lowered hers, directing her attention back to Jide. "Can I see your papers, sir?"

"Sure." Jide reached into the glove compartment and withdrew the documents.

Duke tuned into the surroundings for signs of a threat. The only other sounds were from the police and vehicles on the other side of the highway.

Seconds ticked by and stretched out as the woman perused the car certificates. Finally, she passed the documents back. "Everything is in order. Have a good night."

Jide nodded and drove under the concrete arch, the window sliding up. He blew out a deep breath.

Duke turned to stare out the back window. Satisfied, the cops had set their attention to another vehicle when he saw them talking to the driver, he tipped his head back against the rest and puffed out air.

# TWO

THE NEON lights of Club Arufin came into view, and the car drew up to the alleyway opposite the VIP entrance.

Duke's pulse rate quickened, and adrenaline rushed through him.

What would he find in the tense atmosphere inside? Something to get lost in for a few hours. Preferably a soft, warm body.

"Park the car and come in if you want to. But be ready to leave when I tell you," he said before stepping onto the pavement.

No need for Jide to sit in the car. He would enjoy the scene, too. Some of the other men in his crew were more traditional in their outlooks. Not Jide, though, judging from the porn video he'd once caught the younger man watching, which made him the best choice for the pleasure-seeking trips to Arufin.

The charcoal-walled brick building stood on three levels on the corner of the narrow one-way street. A multi-level car park lay on the adjacent lot. On the other side of the road, bright neon signs, men and women standing in the window displays advertised their fleshy wares. Music and conversations vied for aural dominance.

Two hefty uniformed bouncers flanked the exclusive side archway, while a long queue for the main entrance meandered around the block.

Duke flashed the VIP pass. The doormen tipped their heads in greeting.

He nodded at them and strode into the sleek lobby lit by spotlights.

"Welcome to Club Arufin, sir. Card, please." A dark-skinned guy in a grey shirt sat behind a glass counter and held out a microchip reader.

Duke waved the card, and the device beeped.

The attendant checked his monitor screen. Satisfied, he smiled. "The VIP Lounge is on the next level up, through those doors, sir."

"Thank you." Duke strode down a short hall and pushed the door into the lounge. The sights and sounds enveloped him as he stepped into the space packed with revellers. Strobe lightings streaked across the main dance floor with bodies gyrating to loud thumping music.

Instead of heading up to the next level, he made his way to the bar. The crowd parted quickly. He wasn't the largest man in the building. But with a confident stride, he made eye contact with everyone in his path. No one misread his no-nonsense expression.

At the bar, he ordered brandy, swallowed a sip, and took the curved stairs up to the VIP lounge. Men and women sat on dark leather sofas in sections with an empty space reserved for dancing. He found a single-seater armchair in the corner, his back to the wall.

He never liked sitting in a room with his back exposed. He preferred to see trouble before it found him. Problems were never far away, weekend break or not.

Male and female dancers in nothing but sparkling tasselled thin scraps of fabrics that left nothing to the imagination gyrated on raised, caged platforms dotted around the club. Sweat and glitter making their toned bodies glisten.

After tossing back the shot, he caught the eye of a young waiter who sauntered over and took the refill order. While waiting, he checked out the talent on offer.

A group of three thirty-something-year-old women sat in the next section. Two of them looked like a couple by the way they touched each other.

The third met his gaze and flashed a set of white teeth. Arching her brow and lifting her hand, she enquired if she could come over. She was good-looking with long dark-brown hair and a dress that hugged every part of her slender body, boobs nearly spilling out of the low décolletage.

Duke tried to picture holding her woman face down, legs spread wide as he fucked her over the table. His dick gave an unenthusiastic twitch. He was still too tense to entertain company. With a shake of his head, he dissuaded her from getting up. The woman shrugged and tipped her drink in salute.

The waiter brought the refill. He took a sip and relaxed into the leather chair, welcoming the gentle alcoholic haze in his mind that stripped the agitation away. His gaze trawled, exploring every female form.

Another group of women sat a few sofas away, young and fresh-faced. Boisterous, they talked and laughed in loud voices, drawing attention.

Duke spotted her and his world tilted.

The woman was whispering something to the person sitting next to her when her long dark lashes fluttered upwards in a slow, teasing manner.

Skin prickling, his heart stopped. If he wasn't usually cool under duress, he would've drooled.

The brunette was in her twenties. Cute as hell in a halter-neck copper-coloured minidress with bead embellishments on expensive shiny fabric that clung to a curvy body. Face like a fucking angel, curly brown hair flopped over her face in bangs, and she pouted her red lips the way fashion models did.

Duke had no problem picturing the honey on her knees, her heart-shaped mouth stretched around his girth.

She rose from the sofa, huge, dark eyes shining with amusement and mischief. She swayed in seductive motion to the slow music, gaze fixed on him. Her joyfulness seeped into him, and her laughter kept him spellbound.

It took all his will power to remain rooted in the seat instead of joining her on the dance floor.

One of her friends laughed and lowered her head towards the low table, a rolled note in her right hand.

Columns of white powder lined the glass-topped surface, and the woman leaned over, sniffing half of the line before she straightened and repeated the action with the other nostril. Finally, she tilted her head back, pinching nostrils.

Jaw clenched, Duke averted his gaze. The drug remained illegal but was freely available in Arufin for the right price.

He shouldn't begrudge the young ladies their vices any more than he should condemn himself for seeking sex with strangers. Still, he couldn't help the weight of disappointment that settled on his shoulders. He'd seen the damage addictive drugs could wreck on perfectly healthy lives. He'd taken an oath to keep the toxic substances out of Odili territories. Lori Osa wasn't his turf, and there was nothing he could do other than ignore the women snorting the white powder.

Earth angel sashayed over and stood only inches away, her lips curled in the most gorgeous smile. "Can I buy you a drink?"

Duke's gaze held captivating hazel-brown irises.

For a moment, he forgot his disgust at what he'd seen her friend do and simply admired the specimen of beauty. The flawless skin, the perfect button nose, and the gentle curves of a woman in the process of becoming made him aware of his rapid heartbeat.

Damn. She was delicately beautiful. He hadn't paid attention to women for a long time. Not enough to describe them with such a phrase. He liked them more robust than she looked and not someone he would worry about breaking.

"I've got a drink," he replied in a gruff tone and lifted the glass to his lips. He might as well have been drinking water. His senses homed in on the person in front of him.

Undeterred, she lowered her body in the chair opposite and extended her hand. "I'm Carla. It's a pleasure to meet you."

He stared at the manicured, slender fingers that didn't look as if they'd seen a day's labour, reinforcing the feeling Carla wasn't for him. It didn't stop him from picturing them stroking his skin as his dick sprang to life.

"I didn't invite you to join me," his tone stayed dismissive and relaxed, in contrast to the heat riding his blood.

"You didn't."

"I'm not interested."

"I bet I could make you interested." Carla leaned across and settled her hand on his thigh.

Tingles shot up his leg straight to his balls. Stifling a groan, he stiffened as he fought for control. This honey set his veins alight with little effort, leaving him speechless for a moment. Her lips curled into a seductive smile as if she knew exactly how she made him feel.

The open body posture and bright eyes radiated adoration that made him want to grab her and kiss her. Made him want to take the cutie home and keep her. Never let her go.

Where would that get him or her? Dead, that's where.

The conflicting messages—fuck me, keep me, use me, love me—in her body language made him uneasy. Or maybe it was his own mind misinterpreting her candour. Either way, best to play it safe. He wouldn't fall for the girlfriend trap.

"Move along, little girl," he said in a low, hard voice.

Carla stiffened and sat up straight, withdrawing her hand as if she'd been bitten. "I'm not a little girl. I'm twenty-four."

"Still not my type."

From her wounded expression, she didn't look like someone used to getting rejected.

"Whatever. Your loss." She stood and turned away.

The backless dress showed off flawless chocolate skin and hugged rolling round ass as she walked away in stilettos which made him harder. He tossed the drink back, determined to not regret dismissing Carla. Tonight, was about a hook-up, not a relationship.

Unable to look away, he watched Carla return to her friends. Her laughter had vanished. The knot in his belly registered his regret for contributing to her diminished joy.

He barely knew the woman, and yet he wanted the smile back on her face.

With a sullen expression, she spoke to her friends before heading down the stairs alone and disappearing.

Skin prickling, he rolled the glass of brandy between his hands, working his agitation into the motion.

What was she going to do? She couldn't leave without her friends. It wasn't safe to be alone on the street, in the darkness.

The other option? She would hook up with someone else.

Of course, why else did she come here? This was Arufin. People came here for shameless, hedonistic pleasures.

She stood by the bar below, engaged in conversation with a casually dressed big tattooed man who looked like he could crush Carla in his hands.

Duke shifted in his chair. Did the princess have a death wish or what?

Feeling overheated, he drew the waiter's attention and ordered another drink. A glance in Carla's direction showed her headed towards the exit with Tattoo Guy. The knot in Duke's stomach tightened.  What if the big hairy man hurt her?

When the waiter brought the glass, Duke growled at the persistent agitation in his mind, tossed some notes on the table, and headed for the door.

Why the Hell was he invested in a woman he knew almost nothing about.

Except her name was Carla and when he'd looked into her eyes, he'd seen a lost soul, a soul searching for a home.

Fuck. The woman was trouble.

The warm night enveloped him. People still milled around, smoking weed and chatting. A couple adjusting their clothing stumbled out of a dark alley. He headed in the same direction. The man Carla had followed out didn't look like the book-a-room type of guy.

He didn't go far before he heard Carla's loud, defiant protest.

"I said I'm not interested anymore," her voice trembled.

"You promised us a show. You can't change your mind, girl," a deep male voice said.

"I didn't ask for two of you."

"That's enough from you."

The sound of fabric tearing filled the air, followed by what sounded like a muffled cry.

Duke quickened his steps. The end of a narrow dark alley came into view. In the shadows, two hulking figures leaned over a smaller person. Carla.

"Let her go," Duke said in a steady, low-pitched voice, arms stilled at his sides, fingers flexing.

"Oga, mind your own business. Waka pass." The man Carla had approached in the club straightened to his full height.

A large man, he was broad and built like a wrestler. Same as his friend. Reminded Duke of an old nursery rhyme—Tweedledee and Tweedledum.

One look into Carla's rounded, pleading eyes and Duke stepped into their space. "She is my business. Let her go."

"You dey craze? I say waka pass." Tweedledee growled and charged, swinging his arms.

Duke's reflexes took over. Ducking low, he smashed a fist into Tweedledee's groin. The man grunted in agony and fell with a thud to the ground.

*Whoosh. Wham.* Tweedledum came at him, fists jabbing in methodical motions like a boxer. Jaw clenched in a snarl, Duke avoided his punches, biding his time as he backed towards a corner. He kept his composure while adrenaline flooded his veins. The fools didn't know he'd earned an amateur MMA champion's title as a young student.

The chance came. He stepped wide with his left foot, swung his right leg behind him and kicked back. Tweedledum tumbled. Duke pulled him backwards with his arms and flipped him over his right hip. As the man crashed onto the ground, he corked his hand, ready to deliver a death blow.

"No!" Carla shouted, a terrifying tremor in her voice.

Perhaps she thought he'd kill the man. She wouldn't be far wrong. Duke had no qualms about delivering death to any man who deserved it. And right now, these two earned all they got.

"Please." She sounded more subdued, and her fingers clasped Duke's arm.

The touch electrified him, tendrils of warmth and light reaching the part he'd locked away since his parents' death. His rage waned. He released Tweedledum's neck from the choking hold and retreated from the prone man.

Tweedledum spluttered, coughing as he doubled over. Tweedledee groaned, stumbling to his feet.

"Get out of here," Duke ordered, voice chilly and filled with menace.

The man grumbled as he grabbed his accomplice and staggered out of the alleyway.

With the brutes gone, he focused his attention on Carla, looking her over. Aside from smeared lipstick and tousled hair, she looked intact. "Are you okay?"

"I'm ... fine." Her words seemed to be more bravado than fact, considering her body trembled, her breaths coming in short pants.

He resisted the urge to pull her into a soothing embrace. The last thing she would want after an unpleasant encounter with strangers was physical contact from another stranger.

However, the way she looked at him—the steady eye contact, parted lips, and soft expression—anyone would think he was her hero. He was no such thing.

If Carla hadn't been in the damned alley, there wouldn't have been a need to save her.

Even in the dim, dingy alleyway, she sparkled, a glowing angel—a combination of her smile, bubbly personality and the glitzy dress, rather than any supernatural influences. He would be the moth to her flames and burn.

The whole situation annoyed him. Why was he getting sucked in by this troublesome woman when the club had many who would be hassle-free?

"Are you stupid or something? Why the hell did you follow strangers into an alley?" He allowed his frustration to seep into his words.

She jerked back, eyes bulging, obviously taken aback by Duke's harsh tone.

"I—I didn't expect two of them." She sounded hurt and lowered her gaze.

A vice clamped in his chest. He clenched his hands into fists.

Damn it. He hadn't intended to upset her.

"Look, thank you for your help," she said. "You can go now. I'll be fine."

Dismissal? Fuck that. "You don't get to order me around. I'll go when I'm good and ready.

Those men could be waiting at the corner for you."

Her eyes widened for a moment before she tilted her chin up and took a step away. "As I said, I'll be fine."

"Stop." He couldn't help himself. He couldn't let her go without making sure she got back to her friends safely. Then he remembered what he'd seen earlier. "Are you high?"

She halted but didn't turn around. "What are you, the police?"

Duke huffed. "Hardly. I'm concerned."

Carla swivelled, the seductive smile back on her face. "I appreciate your concern. But no, I'm not high."

"Good." He paused as warmth suffused his chest. "You need to learn some self-defence moves, if you're going to keep picking up strange men."

She corked her hips, hands akimbo. "Are you going to train me?"

She looked him over and tugged her bottom lip with her teeth as if she wanted to take a bite at him.

"No fucking way!" His life didn't include her no matter how much she affected him. No matter how much he wanted to take responsibility for her.

"In which case, I'm heading back to the club. I came out tonight to party, and I'm going to party, one way or the other." She turned away.

"No more partying for you, honey." Before he could process his actions fully, he hauled her over his shoulder in a fireman's lift.

Picking up his discarded jacket, he strode out of the alleyway as Carla's giggles rang into the night.

Why did it feel as if the spoilt princess had him exactly where she wanted?

# THREE

CARLA OWO squealed with laughter at being draped over the stranger's shoulder as he strode through the alleyway like a king. The combination of adrenaline rush and being tipped upside down made her lightheaded.

She didn't care, excited to have won the tussle of wills between them.

The moment she'd seen Mr Dark Dangerous and Decadent—or Triple-D as she'd nicknamed him—walk into the VIP lounge she'd wanted him.

His expensive fitted silk-cashmere suit hugged a hard body, and he exuded a dangerous bad boy aura. He was the kind of man she should avoid, considering her background.

Damn! Drop-dead gorgeous, he was a thirst trap in an ovaries-dancing, I-wanna-have-your-babies kinda way. She hadn't been able to resist checking him out.

He'd come in alone, making him unusual. Men with his aura attracted an entourage.

Then she'd stared straight into mesmerising dark eyes framed by sharp cheekbones, an oval face and a low Afro taper fade haircut.

At first, she'd thought he was looking at one of her friends. Jemima was a stunner and a cover model. Ayo attracted attention because of her tats and mohawk haircut.

Carla had dipped her head, casually sipping her drink, thinking he'd look away if he wasn't interested.

Nope. When she glanced up, his gaze remained on her, hungry and intense.

Her stomach had done flips. She'd stood and danced, hoping he would come over.

He hadn't.

Her heart had dropped. Still, she hadn't been deterred. Some men liked the attention of being chased.

Jemima and Ayo had found the whole thing intriguing and had bet she wouldn't be able to get the sexy man to take her home.

She'd won the bet. Yippee.

Her chest tightened.

Okay. She'd played dirty.

But her latest conquest didn't know it.

No one got hurt, right. It had been a harmless prank.

And she hated losing bets to her friends. So fair play.

She pushed the guilt aside. Getting him proved too intoxicating, too exciting.

Just seeing him take down two large men in the alley with only his bare hands had been so damned hot. Now she wished he would carry her cave-man style all the way to their destination. She needed to get some skin-to-skin action with him soonest.

However, as soon as they exited the dark side street, he deposited her shaky legs onto the pavement.

Shame.

"Don't move," he said in a deep sexy drawl, straightening out his cuffs and dusting off his clothes. Then he pulled his phone out of his pocket.

She ran fingers through her tresses to get them in a semblance of order and gave a mock salute. "Yes, sir."

Obeying orders wasn't her trait. Yet, the only place she wanted to be was right next to this man. She stood perfectly still, regal, like she'd been taught in prep school, purse clasped in hands in front of her body.

Mr Triple-D turned his dark piercing gaze in her direction, one brow raised in a don't-mess-with-me arch.

He looked 30-something but acted older like a man who'd lived through many experiences.

Holy shit! The man was all kinds of sexy, even when he was stern.

Her pulse quickened, and her hands itched to touch him. What would he be like in bed? Anticipation dampened her panties. She turned on the doe-eyed pout that sometimes worked with people when they were cross with her.

He exhaled a sigh, shook his head and pulled a phone out of his jacket pocket.

"Jide, bring the car around," he said, without preamble into the gadget, then stowed it away.

His movements and words were controlled and precise. It seemed he didn't expend unnecessary energy on anything. Like when the men had attacked him earlier, his motions had been minimal and practical, an efficient fighting machine.

He commanded attention—the confident poise of his shoulders, the stunning triangular face framed by short twisty hair and trimmed beard and the amused glint in his eyes, all of it was on point.

"Where are we going?" she asked, eager to get somewhere intimate so she could worship at the altar of this god.

"My hotel." His gaze swept the area, and he didn't seem to miss a thing.

In this part of town, anything could happen. Muggings, abductions, whatever. She always came here with an entourage which reminded her of her friends still in the venue.

She pulled her phone out and sent a message to the group.

*I won the bet. Got him! *laughing, dancing emoji* Off to his hotel.*

Messages pinged back almost instantly.

*Wow! I'm so jealous *disappointed emoji*,* wrote Jemima.

*I can't believe I lost another fucking bet *sob emoji*,* sent Ayo.

*Stop betting against me *stuck out tongue emoji*,* typed Carla.

A sleek, blacked-out SUV drew close to the pavement. A young man not much older than Carla hurried to open the back door.

"Get in," Mr Triple-D said, his voice low and commanding.

With heightened senses and trembling limbs, she climbed into the back seat and slid across.

He joined her in the enclosed space, and the door *thunked* shut. Jide returned to the driver's seat, and moments later, the car drove away from the pavement.

In the dimply enclosed space, silence reigned except for the quiet humming of the engine and air-conditioner.

Her heart raced. She tried not to stare at the man sitting beside her as if he was her next much-needed meal.

Why was he so quiet anyway? Why wasn't he touching her?

She swallowed the lump in her throat and tried not to fidget.

"Do you come to Club Arufin often?" she asked, attempting to make conversation. The silence unnerved her.

"No," he replied with a grunt.

Jide didn't say a word or flick his gaze at her in the rear-view mirror.

Interesting. Her chauffeur wouldn't be quiet. When she wasn't on the phone, they would chat or listen to music on the stereo. She could pull her ear pods from her purse and listen. But she would rather talk to this sexy man.

"My friend and I go there almost every weekend," she tried again, hoping he enjoyed listening to her voice as much as she wanted to hear his. "We're local, so it's our joint. But some other people travel a long way to visit Arufin. Even tourists from different countries, all to have the experience. What about you? Do you live in Lori Osa?"

Triple-D said nothing, his neutral expression unchanged.

Seriously, did this guy never lose his cool?

Carla couldn't be this unruffled to save her life. But if the man wouldn't budge, then she had to shut up and find another way to get comfortable. She shifted until their bodies touched and tugged her legs onto the leather seat.

As if he knew what she needed, he settled his arm around her shoulder.

She relaxed, warmth spreading through her body. There was something deeply satisfying and comforting about having his arms around her body, making her feel safe as if she could trust him. As if she could give more than her body to him.

The quiet reassurance seemed more potent than a thousand platitudes.

She drew in a deep breath and filled her nostrils with his warm, masculine scent. He hadn't been in the club long enough for his fresh smell to be polluted, which reminded her that she'd bagged the best man available.

She snuggled deeper, wanting to burrow under his skin, to mark him, so her scent lingered on him and acted as a deterrent to others.

What was wrong with her? She'd met the man less than two hours ago, and she never got attached to hook-ups?

Because this was a hook-up, right? It couldn't be anything more.

So why was she clinging onto his body and nuzzling him as if she was a cat, hoping he would take her home for keeps and make her purr with pleasure?

Seriously, what was this about?

Yet with all the berating, she couldn't bring herself to untangle from him, couldn't bring herself to pull away.

He was too damned secure and comfortable.

"You finally stopped talking," Mr Triple-D's seductively low voice drew her from her thoughts.

Tilting her head, she met his gaze. Breath caught in her throat, her stomach tightening.

Mr Dark Dangerous and Decadent was smiling—the kind that made his dark eyes sparkle and indented his cheeks with dimples that would charm old ladies.

Then there were those sensuous lips. Lips designed to claim and caress, to cajole and conquer, to whisper words of arousal or comfort.

She was a goner. Heart-racing, panty-melted goner.

How far away was the hotel? Couldn't they get started in the car?

She licked her lower lip, her gaze fixated on his.

He seemed to know her thoughts as the smile turned into a smirk, making her cheeks burn.

Needing to pull it together, she averted her gaze. She wasn't a shy or reserved person. Usually, her in-your-face attitude gave her the upper hand. Not with him. He stripped back her layers with a look that said, 'you're not fooling me.'

Still, she couldn't complain about being in his arms.

At this stage of the evening, other men would've been pawing her exposed skin and trying to get under her clothes. Instead, this one was giving her a cuddle as if she was more than a casual fling. As if they were long-time lovers who knew each other's deepest secrets and fears.

Seemed they both matched in this aspect. If she'd found him on a dating app, she would've swiped right. Definitely.

She didn't know much else about him.

"What's your name?" she asked, smoothing out the hem of her dress.

He hadn't mentioned it when she introduced herself earlier. It shouldn't matter. Sometimes when her hook-ups mentioned their names, she forgot them a few hours later.

She wouldn't forget Mr Triple-D in a hurry. Would he remember her? She would make sure he did. Somehow.

"Let's not get personal, Cara," he replied.

"Hang on. Did you call me Cara? My name is C-A-R-L-A, not C-A-R-A," she said in a huff, annoyed that he'd forgotten her name already. Or was he one of those people who mixed up L and R?

"I know your name. As I said, I don't want us to get personal. So, I'll call you Cara. I prefer it anyway."

Still miffed, she puckered her face in a frown, then shrugged. "Well, if we're not using real names, then I'm calling you Triple-D?"

"Triple-D? Sounds like bra size." He chuckled, a thrilling, sexy sound.

How did he know about women's bras? He'd probably bought lingerie for girlfriends.

A twinge of jealousy burned through her chest and she looked down at her cups. How did she compare to his previous women? Her boobs were nowhere near triple anything.

"I think you mean Double-D." She glanced away, aware she didn't measure up to those either.

"That's a relief. But why Triple-D?" He still sounded amused.

She shrugged again. "When I first saw you, I named you Mr Dark, Dangerous and Decadent. Hence, Triple-D."

A warm palm cupped her cheek, making her turn her head to meet his gaze. "Sounds apt when you describe it that way. I like it."

"You do?"

"Yes. The first two Ds are accurate descriptions, and I hope you'll think of me as the last after tonight."

Speechless for the second time tonight, the humility in his words caught her off balance, just as the panty-melting grin returned to his face.

His admission of being a dangerous man should have her running for the hills. She was surrounded by deadly, sinister men at home. Men she could hardly endure. Men she wanted to escape from. The type of men she should never consider hooking up with or dating.

Here she was still clinging on to him.

For one reason only.

The men in her life were arrogant and boastful and would never admit to any weaknesses.

Triple-D had admitted to not being perfect.

His lack of false pride made her want him more than ever.

Boy, was she screwed.

# FOUR

"CARA, I just told you I was a dangerous man." The gravelly tone of Triple-D's words made his chest vibrate under Carla's cheek.

"I know," she replied, not lifting her gaze., so he wouldn't know the truth about her.

How could she tell him about the dangerous men in her life?

People who knew her were only interested in getting close to her because of her father.

Good thing, he said not to get personal.

"And you're not scared?" he asked, tipping her head up, his tilted to see her face.

"You won't hurt me," she said, looking into his dark, compelling eyes.

Frown lines rumpled his forehead. "You don't know that. You don't know me."

"I know what I've seen of you so far. You came to my rescue when you thought those men would hurt me. And we've been in this car for more than thirty minutes, and all you've done is wrap me in your warm embrace. Those are not things a man would do if he intended to hurt me."

He might yet break her heart, but that was a different matter altogether.

"Hmmm," he huffed in annoyance. "You are a little naïve."

He sounded like the men in her life who always berated her because she wasn't as ruthless as they were.

"It's better to be innocent than to be wicked. If hurting me is your intent…" she trailed off and looked away, suddenly overwhelmed by emotions, tears backing up behind her eyeballs. Perhaps this was a bad idea after all. "Stop the car."

"Jide, pull over," Duke ordered, noticing her distress.

The car came to a smooth stop just before a junction.

Shocked that he'd stopped the car when she demanded it, some of her annoyance dissipated. She moved to sit upright, and Duke released his grip on her. She turned her back to him, a little dismayed about displaying emotions when he didn't want to get personal. She'd never been good with hiding her feelings, something he seemed to have mastered.

"I'm sorry, Cara," he said in a gentle, sincere tone. "I didn't mean to upset you."

She swallowed a few times before she could speak. "Thanks. I'm okay."

"If you would rather go home, we can drop you off. I will be disappointed, but I'll understand."

She sighed and looked out of the window. Taking the right turn would get them to her neighbourhood within a few minutes. However, she wasn't in a rush to face her life. No matter how bad this man was, he couldn't be as bad as the ones who waited for her. "I don't want to go home. How far is your hotel?"

He pointed left of the windscreen. "It's across Bandele Bridge. No more than ten minutes."

"You're staying on Pleasure Island?"

"Yes."

"Then let's hurry."

He didn't look convinced. "You're sure?"

"Yes, come on. I love Idunnu. It's one of my favourite places in the world."

"Okay." He grinned and turned to the driver. "Jide, you heard her."

"Yes, boss." Jide turned left at the traffic lights and drove onto the well-lit bridge.

She relaxed into the leather seat and snuggled into Triple-D's hardness. Anticipation sizzled in her veins.

Within minutes, the car stopped in front of the crescent-shaped exclusive five-star Idunnu Hotel, and a uniform-clad doorman opened the door.

"Wait in the car for a minute," Triple-D said before stepping out.

Instead of following, Carla stayed as he'd instructed, watching him.

He swept his gaze across the entrance and the driveway leading to the road as if he searched for something. As if he knew what she'd done.

A shiver passed through her and goosebumps mottled her skin. She'd done a stupid thing earlier. Was she about to be burned by the consequences?

Finally, Triple-D opened the door wide. "Come on."

He hurried her up the short steps of the hotel, through the marbled lobby, and into a lift. Her blood bubbled, and the doubt fizzled away. She hadn't been caught out. His actions weren't of a man about to kick her ass for the stunt she'd pulled tonight.

Instead, he acted as if he couldn't wait to have her all alone. Couldn't wait to sate the intense need glittering in his dark eyes.

In the enclosed space of the boxcar taking them up to his hotel room, he didn't breach the gap between them.

Gosh, he was very proper, very well mannered. The kind of man her mother would've loved for her if she were alive.

Her heart squeezed tight, and she shook her head. She wasn't going to think about Mummy. Not tonight.

As a distraction, she moved close to her new sexy man and covered the massive bulge in his trousers with her palm. She wanted him badly, wanted him wrapped around her, filling her up, making her forget the ugliness of her life.

He gripped her wrist and moved it aside.

"Behave yourself." The tone of his voice lacked any venom, and his eyes sparkled with amusement.

"Spoilsport." Lips pouted, she settled against the cold, shiny metal enclosure.

He chuckled. A warm sound that vibrated inside her.

Boy, she loved the sexy sounds he made, whether he was just talking or laughing. Loved the way his deep black eyes glittered.

His handsome face lit up with his laughter, contrasting with the intensity he exuded from the moment she'd seen him at the club. She wanted to luxuriate in his presence even when he wasn't touching her.

The lift pinged, and she stepped out first into the bright corridor.

"You're eager," he said and followed her out.

She stared at his groin and licked her lips. "You bet I am."

Chuckling, he opened a door, flicked on the light, and stepped into the suite, looking it over before allowing her in and clicking the latch shut behind her.

The suite was sophisticated, modern, and on the high end with the vaulted ceiling, chandeliers, and luxurious furnishings.

"Nice," she said. She'd spent her twenty-first birthday weekend in this resort, so she knew what to expect.

He laughed as she walked past him toward the bedroom. When her gaze connected with the mirror on the ceiling over the humongous bed, she gasped. "Wow. You like watching."

"Among other things. Come here," he said in a husky voice.

A delicious tremor went through her at the authority in his voice. Compelled, she swivelled and sashayed back to him. She pressed her body against his. Seconds later, she was flat against the wall, hands pinned above her head, facing the silver-charm brocade wallpaper.

"Be still." His words whispered across her nape.

Left breathless, her heart thundered. A warm palm slid up her side, roamed her body, and covered the right bum cheek through the dress. She shivered. Not from cold. With the fresh controlled air in the room, her body still burned up from the inside. Something about this man pushed all her buttons.

At the club, everyone around had noticed him. Her friends had talked about him. Yet, no one had approached him except her. He had an air of danger around him, and he'd already proven it in the alley.

He was prepared to take a life to save hers. He'd been ready to take her home if she'd wanted to go, without getting anything in return.

If she weren't already in lust with him, she'd fall deep, knowing he would do anything to protect her. Nobody in her life offered the same level of physical and emotional security without asking for something in return.

She wanted to give him something, something he would hopefully remember.

Her body trembled with excitement, as her core contracted in anticipation of him inside. She pushed hips back, rubbing her bum against his hard bulge.

His hands left her body, and she missed his heat immediately. Swivelling, she found him taking his jacket off.

"You're not very good at following instructions," he said without looking at her.

"I don't usually have to work so hard to get what I want." Smirking, she stepped forward, intending to help him undress quickly.

"Don't come closer."

That voice again. Quiet. Assured. Powerful. Any resistance she had melted. Her body stilled in obedience.

He gave her the once over. Heat skittered over her skin as his gaze trawled her body.

"So, you always get what you want?" His voice was a husky, sensual rumble, adding to the electricity zapping the air between them. His long fingers undid the buttons of his shirt, revealing more skin she wanted to lick.

"Mostly," she said with a sigh.

She had the things money could buy. However, she wanted her mother back in her life most of all, and she hadn't met anyone who could resurrect the dead.

"Well, honey. Tonight, I get what I want." He removed the cufflink from his left arm.

It seemed he was performing a striptease for her entertainment without the music or the choreographed hip movements.

Mesmerised, her gaze followed his movement. "And what's that?"

"You." His mouth tilted in a delightfully sexy grin and he slid the other cufflink off.

"Oh." Her heart thumped.

"Do me a favour. Take your clothes off while I run the bath, will you." He winked and strode into the bathroom.

Oh, he was something else. Wow.

Her mouth popped open and close a few times like a goldfish. She turned into a quivering mass, almost a puddle because of his sensual promise. With trembling hands, she reached up and unclipped the halter end of the dress.

She imagined sitting in the bath, surrounded by fragrant water and the cocoon of his body—an erotic and romantic experience, considering this was a one-night stand. At this rate, she wouldn't want the night to end.

In a haze of lust, she shimmied out of her dress, removed her underwear and flung the clothing over the back of one upholstered armchair. Then she unstrapped and kicked off her stilettos.

She straightened, heart slamming against her ribs.

He leaned against the doorpost, devoid of his shirt and shoes, hands shoved in his trouser pockets.

Jeez, the man was hot. The glint in his black eyes, the hard planes of muscles, the whorls of short dark hair and ... scars on his torso, all indicated she'd made the right choice. He would give her what she needed tonight. No holds barred.

He whistled, the sound reverberating around the room. His gaze latched on to hers as he demolished the space between them. "You're fucking beautiful, Cara."

Speechless, warmth spread across her chest. Her heart thrummed like a hummingbird. She forgot everything else—to breath, her nakedness—and got lost in the sexy intensity of his eyes. Eyes seemingly full of admiration, adoration for her.

One palm cupped her face, thumb trailing along her neck, sending tingles down her spine. The other hand jammed into the tight curls on her nape, tugged her head back, as he lowered his.

His lips were soft. Full and soft. His tongue explored her mouth. Hungry. Seeking. Savouring.

She moaned, grabbed his bare back and rubbed against his hardness. Her nipples tightened, her breasts were weighted and tender.

He broke the kiss. Nibbled the corner of her mouth. Nuzzled her chin and neck. Bristles scoured her sensitive skin. Callused hand travelled over her contracting belly, stroked the seam of her labia and met slick, slippery surface.

She gasped for air, leaked like a tap. A thumb swiped her clit and fingers spread the moisture, teasing, before surging inside her.

Her body caught fire and trembled. He nipped her shoulder, stubble scratching her skin. She rode his rough palm, his digits pumping in and out.

"Oh...Oh...I'm going to come." The words rushed out of her, a warning.

He released his grip on her back and slid to his knees. Like an acolyte ready to worship at her altar, he hooked her left thigh over his right shoulder, opening her up to his waiting mouth.

"I'm going to taste you," he said before he sucked her clit, while two of his fingers fucked her.

She hadn't thought a man in this position could be powerful until she detonated with an orgasm that made her quake and scream. When she would tumble over, he scooped her up and carried her into the bathroom.

# FIVE

HAZY SUNSHINE filtered through the heavy drapes. Duke stared at the sleeping woman beside him in bed. The fact that he'd allowed her to stay overnight rolled in his brain. He'd broken plenty of his rules with Carla.

No innocents.

No intimacy beyond fucking.

No overnight stays.

All broken.

On the ride back to the hotel last night, he'd come to a realisation. His agitation had dissipated. He couldn't remember the last time he'd been relaxed both physically and mentally. Although he'd nearly maimed two men over the night.

His current state of calm could be attributed to the great sex they'd enjoyed rather than the woman. Sex was supposed to be therapeutic, after all.

Still, he relished the warmth and softness of Carla's body against his, more than he'd done with anyone else. Beyond their physical attraction, the mix of her boldness and ingenuousness added a layer of feelings he hadn't experienced previously. The brash way she'd approached him in the night club had contrasted with the naivety she'd displayed in the car when she'd said he wouldn't hurt her. How could she trust him so easily?

In his world, trust was a highly valuable commodity and not so easily given, and certainly not with someone intended to be discarded after a few hours.

His initial reaction to her statement had been annoyance because he wanted her to be savvier, more discerning, more cautious.

However, the fact that she trusted him filled his heart with warmth and took him to a plane of self-awareness he hadn't experienced with other lovers. Gaining her trust made him want to be the best man he could be for her, even for the short time they would spend together.

Absently, he stroked down her arm, inhaled deeply, taking in her scent of lavender, and vanilla, a perfect blend of sensuality and sensitivity. Just like the woman in his arms.

He needed to send her on her way but couldn't let her go. Yet. A few more hours with her shouldn't hurt.

Something about last night prickled his mind. Grabbing his phone and trousers, he got out of bed and headed to the bathroom. Door shut, he leaned against it, pulled on the pants, and made the call.

"Kedu nke na-eme?" His friend, Mason, asked after a ring as an image of him projected on the screen. He was in a T-shirt, sitting up in bed. The call had probably woken him up. In their line of work, they kept late nights and slept through the mornings sometimes.

"Ọ nweghị ihe na-eme." This simple Igbo greeting between them was a way of clearing the line and letting the other know it was safe to talk. "Any news for me?"

"Nothing new. Are you still back tomorrow?"

"Yes. As scheduled."

It was never safe to discuss business on the phone. Some technologies made it easy to eavesdrop on conversations. He couldn't risk sensitive information getting into the hands of ruthless people who would misuse it.

"I need you to run a check on a number plate for me," he continued and read out the digits from memory.

"Hold on," Mason said and got out of bed, the image showing the dimly lit bedroom, the blinds on the windows still closed. He placed his phone on a stand, pulled up a laptop and swiped his fingers across the monitor several times. The screen came alive with images and texts.

Don Sylvester Odili, the family patriarch, had ensured that all the potential heirs to Odili Enterprises had received formal educations against the traditional route of informal apprenticeships.

Duke had acquired an MBA while Mason held a degree in Computing, hence their job titles as CEO and CTO, respectively.

"Bingo!" Mason said when an image was selected. "It's registered to—" he typed quickly. It looked like he was hacking into the car registration servers. "—Mr Bola Akindele who lives in Lori Osa, according to his driving licence."

The hairs on Duke's nape stood erect. "Did you say Lori Osa?"

"Yes, that's what it says on here. I'm sending the details to your device now." He screwed up his face. "Is there something I should know?"

Except for the coincidence of Mr Akindele living in his current location, there wasn't anything to know. Duke didn't want to get anyone worried over nothing.

"Last night, I thought we were being followed. After we arrived at the hotel, the car drove past. Nothing happened."

Except that he'd picked up the most beautiful woman. He wouldn't mention Carla, though.

"You know I'm not happy you've only got Jide on site." Mason had a frown on his face. "I can send a couple of men, and they'll be with you in thirty minutes max."

They had associates and resources in Lori Osa they could tap into if required.

"No. Don't do that. As I said, it was nothing." Other men coming here meant broadcasting

Carla's presence. He didn't want to expose Carla to his shit. And he wanted to enjoy the bliss of this day without worries of his past or business matters.

Mason stared at him as if he would argue and nodded instead. "So, I hope you managed to get your freak on last night. From the grin spreading on your face, I'd say you did."

"I'm not going to discuss my sex life with you, Mace," he used the other man's nickname. "Have a good day."

He switched off the cell and stared at the mirror over the sink. He was grinning. In fact, he'd had a grin on his face since last night. Since Carla.

Not wanting to overanalyse the reasons the woman made him happy, he stripped off and stepped into the shower.

After a quick wash, he applied lotion, wrapped a towel around his waist, walked over to the sitting room, and ordered breakfast.

Carla strode over, wrapped in a fluffy white hotel robe, her hair a halo of tight ringlets around her face.

His heart lurched in his chest.

She looked like an angel—his earth angel.

He returned the phone handset to the cradle and leaned bum against the table. "You are a gorgeous sight to behold."

A smile lit up her face. She glided across the carpet to him, then stood between his thighs. "I missed you in bed."

A fist clutched his heart and squeezed. He'd never had a lover say those words to him. He tugged her shoulder with one hand, tilted her head up with the other, and slanted his lips across hers. Her taste exploded in his mouth. Sweetness he couldn't seem to get enough of.

He hardened instantly and physically ached for her. Wanted to spend the rest of the day savouring every part of her even after the night of hot, fulfilling sex they had.

Breaking off the kiss, they both gulped in air. His rigid dick pressed against Carla's hip. He tilted her face, brushing his mouth on her cheek and jawline. Nipped the smooth skin and then soothed the sting with his tongue.

He explored her skin with lips just as she traced his back with fingers. Her touch increased his lust. He tugged her closer, aligning their bodies. They were a perfect fit, her soft curves to his hard muscles, her sweetness a balm for his troubled soul.

"Damn it, you drive me crazy," Duke muttered in a husky voice he could barely recognise.

She smiled that bewitching smile of hers and went down on her knees, loosening the towel in the process. Fresh air kissed his dick before her warm, soft palm wrapped around his length and squeezed.

"Carla," he groaned, legs weakened.

When he went to the club last night, he hadn't been looking for someone like Carla. He hadn't expected to bring her back here or to have her stay the night. This morning, he couldn't picture anyone else doing this to him. He wanted her mouth around his cock.

Carla's hand slid up and down his length in firm strokes right down to the base and back up to the swollen slick tip. Her thumb ran over the slit, spreading the drop of pre-cum gathered there.

Pressure built in Duke's balls, the pit of his stomach tightening. Surprised, he let out another groan. He never allowed anyone this much freedom with his body, always controlled everything. Yet, he resisted the urge to grab Carla's head and ram his shaft down her throat.

Drifting a hand to her head, he tangled fingers into the curly mass of hair. He stared at the woman at his feet, breath held in anticipation as she parted her lips. His dick throbbed, twitching in reflex at the warm fan of her breath.

Carla looked up through the curtain of dark lashes and smiled, teasing him.

Damn. She was irresistible—so angelic and seductive at the same time.

He was in trouble. He'd been in trouble since he set eyes on her.

His grip on her hair tightened and his hips rocked forward, nudging the smooth head against her parted lips.

"Suck me," he commanded in a low and rough voice while he fought to maintain control.

Her smile widened. She took his length into her moist, heated mouth.

His whole world converged at this moment. Nothing else mattered but Carla's lips and tongue on his shaft. He fought the urge to take over, to thrust, to thoroughly corrupt this earth angel.

While this was a brief fling—his chest constricted at the thought—he could not bring himself to ruin her, to treat her the way he would treat a casual score.

She had entrusted herself to him. Once trust was given, his code of honour dictated that he could not break it.

Another groan left him. He squeezed his eyes shut and tilted his head back, letting Carla do something he'd never allowed any of his previous lovers to do—to set the pace and control his body and consequently his orgasm.

He didn't care. He opened his eyes. Seeing his moist cock sliding in and out of her swollen lips while she was on her knees was the hottest thing. To top it off, she stroked her pussy with her free hand.

Her hand fisted at the root of his shaft, she bobbed her head back and forth, increasing the pressure and the rhythm.

Pleasure built in his balls, making them draw tight into his body.

The sound of her moan vibrated around his dick just as she came, which became his undoing.

"Fuck!" He exploded, semen spurting out in hot jets onto her mouth and face in an endless moment. He gripped the table, glad to have it as support for his weight.

When he caught his breath, he shifted over to a chair and picked the discarded towel.

"Come," he said.

In response, she crawled across the carpet with catlike fluidity and his lust reignited.

He groaned. "If you carry on like this, you're going to be the death of me."

"You sound like an old man." Her giggles tinkled like merry bells and filled him with warmth, liquifying his bones. She stopped in front of him.

"I can't seem to think of anything else but fucking you." He helped her up and cleaned her with the towel.

"Is that such a bad thing? Fucking me?" she asked in a sultry voice as she climbed onto his lap and tucked her head against his shoulder, getting comfortable.

He wrapped his arms around her. The gesture had become second nature since he met her. "Well, yes. A man can't spend his life in bed."

Or attached to a woman. Mace would tease him if he ever mentioned his reluctance to be separated from this woman whom he only met a few hours ago.

"I guess not." She sounded disappointed.

He placed his fingers under her chin and nudged so she would lift her head. "Surely you don't want to spend the whole day in bed with me. Don't you have anywhere else to be today?"

Big brown eyes stared back at him, as intoxicating as brandy. He resisted the urge to dive back into the decadent pleasures of her body.

She lifted her shoulders nonchalantly. "No, I don't."

Curiosity got the better of him. "Isn't there someone expecting you home? Someone you need to call to say you're okay?" A parent? Housemate? Boyfriend?

The thought of her with another man cut him like a knife. He brushed it aside. He wouldn't go there.

She shifted, averting her gaze. "Erm. It's okay. I'll call them later."

He frowned as unease prickled his scalp, and his stomach curdled.

Did she do this frequently? End up with strange men all night long? Enough for no one to care about her whereabouts.

A knock sounded at the door, distracting him from the unsettling thoughts.

# SIX

"THAT'LL BE breakfast," Duke said in a brusque voice and moved Carla over to the sofa, glad to have some space between them. "Call whoever you need to call and tell them you're fine."

She met his gaze with searching eyes, puffed out a breath and nodded.

Satisfied that she would do as he instructed, he went into the closet and pulled on trousers.

When he came out, Carla was in the bathroom, talking to someone on the phone. For a moment, he stood by the closed door. He could listen in to both sides of the conversation. He had an app which allowed him to eavesdrop on other phone conversations. He'd done it to others many times, all part of staying alive in this business.

This morning, it felt wrong to snoop on Carla. Wanting to find out more about her implied there was more to them than just sex.

So, he strode to the suite door and let in room service. The uniformed man pushed in the trolley and laid out the food on the table.

Duke tipped in cash and shut the door once he left just as Carla came out of the bathroom, dressed.

It was a shame to see her covered. However, he needed to cool his libido so he would think and eat.

Smiling, he swept his arms in an exaggerated motion. "Breakfast is served."

She sashayed over and made to pull out a chair.

"No. Sit on my lap."

She settled on him, and he proceeded to feed her, first slices of melon and grapefruit, then pieces of plantain pancakes. Watching her chew and swallow every morsel became a lesson in control as his libido rose.

At one point, he licked a drop of maple syrup from the corner of her mouth. She fed him a few bites and giggled when he nibbled her finger playfully.

She dabbed a sticky digit on his cheek and then proceeded to swipe her tongue over it. They spent a few minutes kissing leisurely.

Their interactions were natural as if they'd known each other months rather than hours.

The warmth spreading through his body, the wide grin on his face and feeling ultra-awake spoke of his continued elation in her presence. He wasn't ready to let her go.

"What do you think about us spending the rest of the day together?" he asked.

The smile on her face could light up a soccer stadium. "I thought you'd never ask. Yes, I'd love to spend the day with you."

She hooked her arm around his neck and pressed a quick kiss to his lips.

"Good. For clarity's sake. It is just for today. Tomorrow I'm on a flight back home, and I won't be visiting Idunnu for a long time."

"Yeah. Of course, I know that. You have your life. I have mine," she said with bravado, although disappointment flashed in her eyes before she lowered them. "This is just one long-ass one-night stand."

"Do you have them often?" The question slipped out without much thought.

"What?"

"One-night stands. Do you have them every weekend?"

She gasped and stared at him, incredulously.

Perhaps he shouldn't have asked the question. However, now, he wanted an answer. He didn't like the thought of her in a different bed every weekend. Or in an alleyway.

Memories of how he'd rescued her returned. His back muscles tensed and his grip on the fork tightened. He didn't want her going back to that routine any time soon.

She averted her gaze. "My friends and I like to party. It is just sex. No big deal. What about you? Do you have a different lover every weekend?"

It took him a few heartbeats to switch his brain from formulating a plan to get her addicted to him, to forming a reply to her question.

A man in his line of work couldn't afford vulnerabilities. During sex was one of the times when a man was at his most unguarded. A knife in the throat, bullet in the chest or poison in a drink had sent unsuspecting lotharios to their graves. He wasn't about to join them just for the sake of getting his freak on.

He was very selective about his sexual partners. The encounters were brief wham-bam-thank-you-ma'am-type affairs. He rarely took his shirt off, let alone anything else. And those liaisons were so infrequent several months went by between them.

"No, I don't fuck around," he replied. He certainly didn't go down on his knees in front of random strangers like he'd done last night. Carla's was the first pussy he'd tasted in a long time.

The tension in her body dissipated, and she relaxed into him. "Can I see you after this weekend? Perhaps visit you?"

"That's not a good idea."

"You're not married, are you?"

"No, I'm not interested in marriage."

"Look. I'm not looking for marriage either. But we can have a regular arrangement, for times that suit you, if you want."

"You want to be my mistress?"

"I prefer girlfriend. But mistress works too."

The idea of Carla as his mistress, at his beck and call, left him breathless with its appeal. But his concern remained. Anything other than casual hook-ups amounted to a relationship. Relationships were costly and time-consuming. He hadn't met anyone worth the risk. Never mind his inability to be emotionally available.

The knot in his gut tightened.

Was Carla worth the risk?

"You don't understand. My life is not appropriate for relationships."

"Oh, well." She sighed, reached across to the bowl of melon slices, picked a piece and took a bit out of it. Then she slid off his lap. "I guess I better go and do the walk of shame."

His chest tightened, and his heart raced. He wasn't ready to see her go. "You don't have permission to leave."

She stopped beside the chair where her stilettos lay strewn, a frown marring her face. "Permission? I don't need your permission to leave."

"If you were mine, you'd have to do what I say," he hardened his tone and raised a brow, challenging her. Of course, she could leave if she really wanted to.

Duke suspected this was a kind of negotiation to see how much she could get him to relent. He was willing to play along.

Her eyes widened, and the pulse at the base of her neck beat fast. Then she licked her lips. "What would you do?"

He raised a brow. "If you were mine for the day, I'd take you out, get you pampered and treated like a princess. Afterwards, I'd take you to dinner, so you'll enjoy some of the best cuisines in the world. Later, much later, I'd bring you back here and rock your world, one intense orgasm at a time."

A tremor passed through her as she gave him an incredulous stare. "In order words, you plan to ruin me for every other man."

When she said it like that, he had to admit the truth. "You've got that right, Cara. By the time, this weekend is over, I don't want you going back to those casual hook-ups."

"And yet, you won't let me see you after the weekend."

He exhaled a heavy breath. "You might decide you don't like intense orgasms after our time together."

"Never gonna happen," she bit back, hands akimbo.

"Okay." He raised both hands in defeat. "Let's make an interim deal. If you're not fed up with me by Sunday morning, we'll make a longer-term arrangement."

He would worry about what would happen afterwards when they got there.

"Deal." She corked her hips to the left, her seductive smile back in place. "But if I'm going to be here until tomorrow, then I need new clothes."

"No problem. The resort has a boutique." He went to the closet and took his laptop out of the safe.

When he returned to the living room, they spent the next few minutes picking out clothes from the shop website.

She complained about all the different items he added to the basket. Her reluctance to spend his money made him give her a thorough kiss.

Afterwards, he sent her to shower while he picked out jewellery, lingerie, shoes, swimsuit, day and evening wear. She didn't need all those things for the next twenty-four hours, but they would be keepsakes she would remember him by.

He got dressed before the boutique delivered the items and Carla came out of the bathroom.

"Wow. That's a lot of clothes." She stood mouth agape, eyeing all the bags.

"All for you, Cara."

"It all seems a bit excessive." Her expression puckered.

"You're worth every bit. This is my way of saying 'thank you' for agreeing to spend the weekend with me, especially since you know nothing about me."

"Okay. So, what do you want me to do now?"

"Get dressed. We are going to act like the tourist I'm supposed to be."

She opened the bags and flicked out items, before settling on a teal and orange Ankara sundress.

While Carla dressed, Duke sent a message to Jide.

*Going out. Don't need the car. Stay close but not visible.*

*Sure, Boss,* he sent back.

Afterwards, they headed out. They left the hotel and strolled down the promenade.

Carla reached across, and Duke took her soft hand in his—the first time he held hands in public with a girl since he left high school. Seemed like a lifetime ago.

"I love the beach. You know, my mum used to take my brother and me when we were little. We would play with other kids and build sandcastles." She shoved her free hand into the pocket of her dress, her eyes acquiring a faraway glaze.

For a moment, they stood side by side on the edge of the walkway, listening to the waves crash against the sands, the world in motion around their stationary bodies.

From the moment Duke had met Carla, and in the little time they'd spent together, she had always been energetic, talkative and full of life.

Some memory must be weighing her down and keeping her still now.

Duke squeezed her hand in reassurance, to take away the sadness that seemed to hover over her. For a man who didn't want to get personal with her, he was hyper-aware that the line was starting to blur.

"I remember coming to the beach as a child too," he said in the way of conversation to cheer her up.

"No freaking way, man." She glanced at him, and her eyes twinkled with mischief, her body animated again. "Mr Dark, Dangerous, and Decadent had been a child who played with sandcastles? I imagined you came out fully grown, wearing a tailored silk-cashmere suit, a pair of alligator skin shoes, and sporting a handgun in your back strap."

She winked before running towards the shore, her movements playful.

Duke chuckled and tilted his head to watch her. Her observations about him were on the money.

Following Carla onto the sand, he strolled to the bar, which was no more than a grass hut where the barman offered cocktails. He ordered two and took them down to a couple of sun loungers under a white umbrella.

Carla ran up, and Duke handed her a drink before sitting down.

She took a sip. "Mmmhm. Sex on the Beach. How apt." She chuckled before taking another big sip and settling on the other lounger. "Except, I've never had the real thing."

"The real thing?" he asked as he stretched out his legs, relaxing back.

"Yeah. I've never had sex on a beach before. I'd like to try it." She wiggled her brows.

His dick perked up, showing its interest, and he stifled a groan.

This was an adult only beach, as was the resort. Along the sand lay couples in various stages of carousing although he couldn't see any full-on sex acts. He pictured bending Carla over the white plastic table and having his way with her.

"I'm not going to fuck you out here in broad daylight, Carla."

"How about we come back later tonight?" She winked.

He laughed again. "Do you mean you'd rather forgo the comfort of a luxury hotel suite for the option of getting sand in all the wrong places?"

She giggled. "When you put it like that it sounds uncomfortable."

"It can be uncomfortable."

"It's also an adventure, and it's exciting to think someone might catch us."

"So that's your kink. You like the thrill of the forbidden. That's why you visit Club Arufin. That's why you approached me." He suddenly saw her in a whole new light. His angel wasn't all that innocent.

"You've got me. As soon as I saw you, I knew you were a dangerous man, and I just had to have you." There was no shame in her words. Just facts.

He needed to digest her words, so he chose a distraction.

"Come on. Let's go and get some lunch. There's a nice cafe not far from here."

They left the glasses on the table and strode back up the beach to the pavement. His back prickled with the sensation that he was being watched. It had happened last night as Jide drove them back to the hotel. Now, the feeling grew strong. Although this time, it could well be Jide.

His phone pinged, and he pulled it out of his pocket. It was a message from Jide.

*You have a tail. What do you want me to do about it?*

*How many?*

*Two.*

*Keep them in your sights but don't do anything unless they make a move.*

*Got it.*

"Is there a problem?" Carla asked when he put the phone away. They stood in front of the cafe.

"Nothing to worry about," Duke said. "Grab a table and wait for me. I won't be long."

"Okay," she said and sauntered into the shop.

Duke watched her through the window before strolling down the street. He took the next right and doubled back at a sprint, rounding the corner as a man peered into the window of the coffee shop. Something about him was familiar. Duke reached for the gun tucked inside the jacket and strode to him.

"Don't move," he said and jammed the gun hidden by the flap of the jacket into the man's back.

His muscles stiffened. This close, he finally recognised Tweedledee although he was dressed differently from last night.

Duke's hand clenched around the gun and the muscles on his neck corded tight.

Was this asshole still following Carla? Did he plan on finishing what he'd started last night? Somehow, Duke knew he couldn't be alone.

"Where is your friend?" he snarled in a low voice.

Tweedledee stiffened and Duke rammed the muzzle of the gun into his back.

"Talk before I put a hole inside you."

"He—he's in a car parked down the street."

Duke shoved the man's shoulder, keeping the gun to his side. "Move."

They walked about a hundred yards until he nodded at a black car parked in a spot. Across the road, Jide watched the proceedings ready to intercept if Duke got into difficulties.

"Open the back door and get in. Move over to the end."

Tweedledee obeyed, and Duke followed him in, gun still pointing to his side.

"What took you so—" Tweedledum turned from where he sat behind the wheel, and his mouth dropped open.

"I thought I made it clear last night I didn't want any of you near Carla. Do you want to die?" Duke said in a harsh no-nonsense voice.

"It's not what you think," Tweedledee replied in a harassed tone.

"Someone better start talking, or I swear I'm going to put holes through both of you right here. Why are you following Carla?"

"His name is Carla Owo, and we're her bodyguards."

# SEVEN

THE MOMENT Jide entered the restaurant, a cold finger slithered down Carla's spine.

Something was wrong.

She shuffled around to get out of the brown leather-covered bench she had settled in and stood.

"Jide, where is Triple-D?" she asked, meeting him in the aisle.

His face puckered in a frown. "Who?"

Her cheeks heated. She had used the nickname she'd made up rather than the man's real name which she still didn't know.

"Your boss. Where is he?" she amended, keeping her voice low so other diners couldn't overhear.

"He sent me to get you." He waved his hand towards the exit, his muscles bunching under his blue T-shirt. "Let's go."

"I can't leave. I'm hungry." She refused to move. "Look, I already ordered, and I want my lemon drizzle cake."

No matter what else was going on, she needed her sugar rush.

Jide huffed, shaking his head. He released her, reached in his back pocket and pulled out a wallet. Then he strode to the counter and slapped some cash notes on it. "I want to pay her bill and make whatever she's ordered to go."

The wait staff took the money, tapped on his screen and said, "Yes, sir."

He went into the back of the café and came out with a parcel which he put into a paper bag. "Here you go, sir. And here is your change."

"Keep the change." Jide grabbed the bag and handed it to Carla, then he steered her towards the exit.

Outside the heat from the sun embraced her, and she tugged down the sunglasses she had perched on her head. Triple-D had bought it this morning along with a whole load of other items she couldn't use up in a day. Like the dress she wore and the matching strappy sandals on her feet.

Remembering the surprise on her face when she'd seen that stack of bags from the boutique, she smiled. Triple-D had been amazing—as a lover, as a person—generous, attentive, protective. Just the kind of man she needed.

Except he wanted a brief fling, only for the weekend. She was intent on convincing him to let them become more.

Then there was the other thing. His life beyond the resort. The reason he didn't want to get involved with her. She had an inkling—the way he carried himself, the weapons at his disposal and the secrecy surrounding him. She wanted to believe that he was in law enforcement, a government agent. However, a fed wouldn't be able to afford the luxury of this resort without being corrupt or being James Bond.

So, was she seriously thinking about going regular with a narc, considering who her father was and what he did for a living?

What if her father was the target and she was bait?

Her stomach tensed as she considered the crazy idea for one second.

Nah. She glanced at Jide, who walked briskly beside her and giggled. These people were not olokpa. Her creative imagination was overworking again.

"So, you never told me where we're going." she said.

"To the hotel," he replied in a crisp tone.

"Is that where he is? Your boss?"

"Yes."

Tired of referring to Triple-D as 'your boss' she asked, "what's his name anyway?"

"Ask him when you see him."

"Men," she muttered under her breath. Her bodyguards were a lot more talkative than this one. "Why did he go back to the hotel?"

"Ask him when you see him."

She lost her temper and halted, hands on hips. "You know I'm talking to you to make polite conversation. That's what human beings do."

Jide's lips twisted in a smirk. "I remember Boss telling you that you talked too much last night."

"That not true. He never said that."

"Didn't he?"

"You can't talk to me like that. I'm his girlfriend." Okay, a white lie. But she was still here after a one-night stand, so it had to count for something.

"Are you?"

"Fuck you! I don't have to stand here and talk to you." She stomped off toward the hotel lobby.

"Hallelujah! Finally." Jide overtook and reached the automatic sliding doors before her.

Chin up, she sashayed past him, towards the lift foyer.

"He's not upstairs. This way." He pointed to the hallway leading toward the conference rooms.

She hesitated, the quiver in her tummy returning. "What's going on?"

She met Jide's gaze.

For the first time, he appeared sympathetic, and his expression softened. He lifted his hands in surrender. "He just told me to bring you over here. I'm sure he'll explain when you see him."

He pointed at a brown solid wood door. "He's in there. Go on."

She didn't move. Why would Triple-D want to meet her here instead of in the suite? And Jide was mysterious with his responses. Did her lover plan a surprise and Jide didn't want to ruin it? Quite possible, right?

She took steps forward and twisted the handle, pushing the door inwards.

The empty space in the middle of the room came into view, chairs and table lined the walls and grey carpets.

As she pushed the door wide, the human occupants came into her line of sight.

Her heart slammed into her chest.

Her bodyguards, Bola and Leke, sat in chairs to the right. They stared in her direction, their expressions unhappy.

A man stood at the other end of the room, face devoid of emotion, feet planted apart. He clasped a gun in his lowered hands in front of him.

Duke.

Her heart took on a heavy, sluggish beat, and she struggled to breathe.

The game was up. Damn.

How did Triple-D find out about her bodyguards? And how did they end up in here?

"Carla, come here," Triple-D's voice was cold, as in arctic winter cold.

She shivered and went to him.

"What's going on?" she tried to sound confident and nonchalant. The tremor in her voice betrayed her.

Triple-D lifted his left hand and gripped the back on her neck tight enough to make her realise he was not unruffled. "Do you know these men?"

Bola shook his head slightly as if telling her to lie. She was tempted to lie and only say she'd met them at the club. After everything Triple-D had done for her, he deserved the truth no matter how ugly.

"Yes."

"How do you know them?"

"They are my bodyguards." She glanced up at him.

"So, what was going on in the alleyway last night?" He looked down, and for the first time, she saw a flicker of hurt and disappointment in his gaze. It was gone too quickly.

Her stomach curdled. Bile rose in her throat. "It was a silly prank. I can explain it."

He dropped his hand from her neck. "You can explain what? That you set me up? That I was the butt of your jokes?"

"I'm sorry. It wasn't like that." She turned to him, ready to plead.

He ignored her. "Go upstairs with Jide, take your stuff and get out of here. I never want to see you again."

"Please. Listen to me." She grabbed his arm, panicking.

He gripped her arm to the point of pain and yanked her forward. The cold anger in his eyes chilled her body.

"Do you think I'm going to listen to a fucking word you say? You think I'm that stupid? That you can fool me twice." His voice was low and menacing as he spoke close to her ear. "Get the fuck out of here, Carla."

He released her, and she stumbled, stretching out her arms to stay upright.

He didn't reach out to steady her, something he would have done if they didn't have this problem.

She wanted to stay and explain. But he would not listen.

The stony expression on his face spelt icy rage. There would be no getting through to him.

Shaking her head, she stalked away in a huff. When she got to the lobby, she stabbed her finger repeatedly on the button until one lift door opened.

Jide sensing her frustration, pressed the number for their floor before she could.

She tilted her chin up and crossed arms in front of her chest. The ride in the lift seemed to take forever. Yet when it beeped and opened, her chest tightened.

Jide went out, strode down the corridor and opened the door to Triple-D's suite.

How come he had a key? He was a bodyguard. Of course, he'd have a key.

Stupid, stupid woman. She growled in frustration as her stomach rolled.

This was really going to happen. Her weekend with Triple-D was going to end like this. She hadn't even lasted twenty-four hours.

She'd found the hottest man in town, and she couldn't even keep him for twenty-four freaking hours.

She couldn't just let it go. There had to be something she could do.

"I'm going to stay here until he comes back. He has to listen to me," she spoke her thoughts out loud.

Jide stared at her incredulously.

"What? You don't have to do anything. Just let me stay. Tell him I refused to leave."

He barked out a short laugh. "Are you fucking insane? Who are you to think that I'm going to get into trouble for you? It's not even as if I tapped that ass."

"Is that what you want?" she snapped angrily, baiting him, desperation making her rock in place. "Do you want to fuck me? Do you want to fuck your boss's girl, is that it?"

His mouth dropped open, and he stared at her as if she was a monster.

Damn. She'd gone too far. She'd let her big mouth get her into trouble again.

Jide shook his head. "You really are messed up, lady."

"Tell me something I don't know."

"And for the record, you're not his girl. Get your mind out of whatever fantasy you've made up. You think you're the first he's had or bought things for?" He kicked the shopping bags stacked in the corner. "Get over yourself, Ms Owo."

His words cut into her like a knife, but she knew how to fight dirty too.

She forced laughter and grabbed her purse. "You seem to forget something. I don't need his money or his shit." She sneered and kicked the bags too. "I wanted him, and I got him. I used him like the fuck boy he is."

The slamming door had her turning around to find Triple-D standing there looking like he was ready to kill someone. He must have heard her rant.

She froze, mouth agape, heart racing. Now, she'd set fire to Hell.

No one said anything for excruciating, slow seconds. Her breaths came out in short pants, and blood whooshed loudly in her ears.

"It's good to know exactly how you feel, Carla," he said finally, holding the door open and not looking at her.

Sighing, she didn't bother responding as she walked out of the door.

# EIGHT

"WHAT THE Hell is going on here?"

The angry, booming voice woke Carla on Sunday morning. She jerked upright, scratching bleary eyes.

Through her hangover-fogged mind, she still recognised the owner of the loud voice who stood at the entrance to her room.

At first, she didn't understand why he looked pissed off.

Then the events of the weekend came flooding back.

Meeting Triple-D at the club on Friday night, tricking him into taking her to his hotel, spending a fantastic night and morning with him, until the big bust-up when he found out about the set-up.

Shit. Her stomach congealed. The hurt and disappointment on his face when she'd told him that Bola and Leke were her bodyguards had filled her with guilt and remorse.

She'd messed up, thoroughly.

But did Triple-D have to be so harsh, kicking her out without hearing her explanation, without forgiving her?

It wasn't as if she'd killed anybody. It was a harmless prank.

And he'd enjoyed spending the night with her as much as she'd loved it. So, what was the big deal?

Triple-D had been the first man who had shown her genuine affection beyond the physical act of sex. The short time they had spent together had been glorious, from the way he'd acted when he'd thought she'd been in danger to the way he'd fed her breakfast and even the sex had been making love. She'd come more times than he had done. He'd made sure of it. And all the items he'd bought for her. When she'd walked out of the hotel suite, she'd only taken her purse and the outfit she was wearing at the time. She'd left everything else including the dress she'd worn to the night club.

Nausea rolled through her. Having him out of her life so suddenly had sent her into a spiral of depression.

She'd screwed up an incredibly good thing. She should have crawled on her knees to beg him. Dammit, hadn't he ever done anything stupid? Surely, he should have given her a second chance. A chance to plead and explain.

First, she'd screamed and ranted in the car, while Bola and Leke drove her home. After she'd gotten home, she'd cried and then called her friends, Jemima and Ayo, who had come over with drinks and blow to cheer her up. She did what she did best, allowed her wild child to roam free and had drowned her sorrows in booze, drugs and sex.

Of course, she'd stupidly forgotten that Daddy would return from his business trip today. However, she hadn't expected him this early.

The room was trashed, and there were two other women under the covers in her bed. Vibrators and dildos were strewn on the comforter, leftover lines of coke dusted the side tables, and bottles of bubbly tipped over the sides.

Her throat felt choked with sawdust. "What is it?"

"You're asking me that?" Her father's steely hazel eyes bore into her. His lips were in a thin angry line. Her father never praised her when she behaved well. In fact, acting up seemed to be the only time she got any attention from him.

"Clean this place up and meet me in my den, Carla," he barked out before walking out of the bedroom.

Shit. This was not her finest moment. Her father had found her in this state. It seemed she was aiming for a world record in screwing up and pissing people off this weekend. Could it get any worse?

Puffing out a heavy breath, she levered up to her elbows and untangled herself from the other still sleeping bodies. Her head hurt like Hell. How much had she drunk?

The moment her feet hit the carpet, her stomach protested, and only pure luck made her reach the toilet bowl in time.

She'd officially hit a new low.

After puking out her guts, she stayed on the cold floor tiles for a long time before she managed to get back on her feet to brush her teeth and shower.

Covered in a towelling robe, she padded into the bedroom to wake her partners-in-crime.

"Ayo." She shook the one closest to her. "Jem, wake up."

Ayo stirred, rolling onto her back. "What is it?"

"My dad is home, and he's mega mad. You have to go."

"Shit." Jemima swung her feet over the side and then held her head as she groaned. She seemed to be feeling the effects of the alcohol too.

Ayo got out of bed without so much as a wince and walked to the bathroom naked. She was androgynous, athletic and covered in tattoos, while her natural locks were shaved at the sides in a mohawk style.

Jem was the opposite with long extensions blended into her straightened hair. She was afraid of needles and would never allow anyone to put a tattoo on her voluptuous figure-eight body.

Carla was somewhere in the middle, with a pear-shaped body, not hardcore enough to shave her head but wild enough to get one tattoo on her leg. Her hair was natural and long as she sometimes alternated between wearing extension-weaves or putting her hair into twists.

They'd been friends for years, came from wealthy families and were generally looked on as non-conforming, which was why they got on with each other.

While Ayo and Jemima got ready, Carla tried to put the place back in some order, tossing stuff into the bin or drawers. They agreed to call her later to check how she got on with her dad before they left.

Dressed in a multi-print maxi dress with a decent neckline and quarter-sleeves, hair held away from her face with a grip and no makeup, she went downstairs. She had already antagonised her father this morning. Best to play the good girl, if she didn't want him to come down on her with a heavy hand.

In the kitchen, the housekeeper greeted her in with a cheery, "Good morning, sunshine."

"Morning, Aunty Dupe," she mumbled and opened the cupboard in search of a glass to take some painkillers.

Dupe was the only decent older female in the household, so Carla deferred to her out of respect.

"I made your favourite. White chocolate and lemon muffins." She pulled out a rack of muffins from the oven.

The sweet aroma made Carla's stomach growl. She curled her lips into a smile as she chased the tablets with water and placed the glass in the sink.

This woman was one of the reasons she lived in this house. One of the reasons she lived. Period. She was a ray of sunshine in an otherwise fucked up existence. She knew exactly how to brighten up Carla's day.

Sunbeams streamed in through the panorama windows, searing Carla's retinas. Her eyes felt like they were being gouged out with a fork. She reached for the sunglasses perched on her head and sighed in relief when the glare was deflected.

Dupe turned the muffins into a dish. Carla walked over, kissed her on the cheek, and made to snag one of the cupcakes.

Dupe smacked her hand.

"No walking and eating," she chastised. "Sit down, and I'll bring a plate over with a cup of coffee."

"Daddy summoned me to his den," Carla protested.

"Your dad can wait a few more minutes while you have breakfast," she replied.

If it had been anyone else, Carla would have argued. But not even Daddy argued with Dupe. A relative on her father's side of the family, she'd been around for as long as Carla could remember, and she wasn't averse to putting Daddy in his place when necessary.

After pulling out a chair at the kitchen table, Carla sat down.

Dupe placed the plate of muffins in front of her as well as a mug of steaming creamy coffee.

As Carla ate the delicious goodies, she thought about Triple-D and how he'd fed her breakfast yesterday while she sat on his lap and swiped the food from his fingers.

Heat flared on her skin. Would she ever see him again?

As she didn't know his full name or have his contact details, finding out where he lived would be near impossible. She could go back to the hotel and ask about him. What would she exactly ask for?

"Oh, do you know how I could reach the Friday night occupant of room 1001?"

The hotel staff would laugh at her.

"I hear you fucked up again." Her older brother swaggered in, cocky as ever, with a smirk on his face.

Fucking great. She groaned out loud.

The perfect son was here to witness her humiliation.

Marlon was Daddy's favourite. As far as their father was concerned, the sun shone out of his ass.

However, Marlon lived a debauched life that bordered on psychotic. But he sucked up to Daddy, so that was okay.

"Good morning, Marlon," Dupe said.

He muttered a response as he walked over to the table, went to snatch muffins from the plate, and got the same treatment Carla got from Dupe. A smack on the hand.

The angry glare he gave her was murderous, and for one moment, Carla thought he was going to punch her.

To be fair to Dupe, she kept her cool and pretended nothing had happened. "Sit at the table, and I'll get your breakfast," she commanded.

"I'm not ten years old," he snapped and grabbed a muffin.

"No. You're not ten. But you'll sit down to eat in my kitchen, or you don't eat at all."

Marlon glared some more but knew better than to do anything against Dupe. She ran the house and kitchen like her personal fiefdom, and their father allowed her the liberty. Marlon held his tongue more out of fear of Daddy than fear of Dupe. Dad would have his hide if he did anything to the woman.

"Grow up, Marlon," Carla said, her annoyance rising at the way he behaved toward the older woman.

Dupe had nursed him, for goodness' sake. Marlon needed to learn some respect. Except, he did not respect anyone.

He mumbled something that sounded suspiciously like "...won't be around forever" as he pulled out a chair and sat opposite Carla with a sneer on his face.

A shiver of dread went down her spine. Had he just threatened Dupe or Daddy? Her brother was twenty-six and full of ambition. One day, he would take over their father's business empire. Was that day looming close?

Suddenly out of appetite, Carla pushed back and stood. "Breakfast was delicious as usual."

"You're welcome." Dupe patted her shoulder.

Carla brushed lips against the woman's cheek. "I better go and face the music."

She didn't want to see Daddy, but she didn't want to sit and watch her ungrateful, annoying brother eat breakfast, either.

"This, I have to see." Marlon's cold laughter followed her as she hurried out of the kitchen.

Her father was one of the richest men in the country. Every time she walked into his den, she felt as if she had travelled back in time to some by-gone era. The room was filled with dark wood and leather. Smelled of those, too, as well as tobaccos he smoked which were hand-made in the old traditional way from Cuba.

To everyone else, Daddy was a legit businessman and political kingmaker. To those in the know, he was the head of the Owo Cartel and nicknamed The Baron. John Bull Owo controlled everything deviant in the region, drugs, prostitution, racketeering. There were no transactions that went through without his getting a cut. You name it, he had a finger in the pie.

Right now, he sat on a sofa watching the monitor screen that flashed news in a ticker at the bottom and had a presenter on the top.

"Take a seat, Carla." He waved at another sofa. His face twisted in a disappointed frown.

Nothing new there. Daddy always seemed to be unimpressed by her.

Except, this time, she'd earned the disapproval.

While she benefited from her father's wealth, there were times when she wished she could have her father's love instead of the money. Times when she wished her mother was still alive. Times when she wanted to join her mother in Heaven if such a place existed.

She lowered her body into the chair and said nothing.

The door to Daddy's den opened, and her brother walked in.

"Good. You are here, Marlon. We can get started," Daddy said.

"What? He has to be here, too?" Carla grumbled.

"Of course," Marlon said with a smirk.

"This is a family matter, and he should hear what I have to say," Daddy replied.

Carla resisted rolling her eyes heavenwards. She was in trouble and didn't need to make it worse.

They were hardly a close family unit. Dysfunctional would be a better description.

Marlon was the son and heir. He and Daddy were inseparable.

Since her father had refused to allow her to work in the profession she'd studied, Performance

Arts, she had refused to work in the family business.

For now, she focused on making amends and sucking up. "Daddy, I'm sorry about this morning."

"You may well be sorry, Carla." He did not sound forgiving. "But we have a problem."

"I know, and I'll fix it," she said, shifting forward in the seat.

"How are you going to do that?" Marlon cut in.

She glared at him and turned to Dad. "Honest, Dad. I'll make amends. I'll reduce the partying."

She couldn't promise to stop them totally. That would be an outright lie.

She still wanted something to fall back on when she needed an escape from her life.

Her father sighed dramatically. His bushy eyebrows drew together, more lines appeared, and a shadow crossed his face. His dark, well-styled hair had salt and pepper strands at the sides. He was a good-looking man even for his mature age and never lacked female company. But the life he led had hardened him, and it showed in his cold eyes.

"This has gone beyond just your partying." He withdrew a cigar and picked up a platinum double-guillotine cutter. "Yes, you need to show some discretion about what you do, where you do it—" He sliced off the curved head."—and with whom."

The fluid motion with which he sliced off the end of the cigar felt like he was slicing off a fingertip. Like he was threatening Carla.

She suppressed a shiver. She had to be imagining it. Daddy wouldn't threaten her, would he?

"You need to do a lot more, Carla. First, there's the business. You need to get more involved."

"Daddy, I don't know anything about this business."

"Then you need to learn," Marlon interjected.

"Yes, you need to learn. This is the business that feeds you and pays for all your partying. It's time for you to start contributing."

Shit. She was waiting until she turned twenty-five and had access to the trust fund her mother had set up. She would move out of this house and open a film production company. Now, this?

Her father had blocked all the jobs she'd applied for. No employer wanted to take on The Baron's daughter and incur her father's wrath.

"With that in mind, your first contribution to the business will be working on a new alliance with one of the northern cartels through marriage," her father continued.

She focused on figuring out employment alternatives, so it took a while to process the words like contribution, alliance and... Marriage.

"Marriage? What are you talking about?" She looked wildly at Marlon who had a sinister grin on his face and back to Daddy who puffed out smoke.

"We are working with the Sani family and looking at merging operations. Marriage between you and Alhaji Sani's son, Abdul, will strengthen ties between us."

"No way. I can't marry Abdul Whatever. I'm not ready for marriage."

Her father's expression hardened, and his voice lost all warmth. "I've been tolerant of your behaviour in the past few years. I know your mother's death was hard on you. But you're not a baby anymore. It's time for you to grow up and contribute to this family like an adult."

"Yeah, okay. You can find something for me to do in the business. But getting married to some guy I don't know? No way, I'm not doing it."

"You don't have a choice anymore. We need you to do this. The Sani deal is particularly important to us, and nothing can derail it."

"This is not the nineteenth century. You can't make me," she huffed.

"Yes, I can. If you don't do this, you'll be cut off from accessing any money."

Not good. Maybe, she'd have to lower herself and do menial jobs, after all. "I'll find a way of earning money."

Marlon laughed harshly. "I'd like to see you find a job. What can you do? No one will employ you."

"Sure, I can." She stopped short of bragging about her blow job technique. This wasn't time for a smart-mouth comment.

"You are not going to have the option of getting a job." Daddy pulled out an A4 manila envelope from a tray and pushed it across the table in her direction. "Go ahead. Look at the contents."

She tipped the envelope over. Glossy photos slipped out, along with paper with printed text. Her heart stopped. The photographs were of her in different sexual positions with different men at various locations. Some of them would have been months ago as she couldn't even remember some of the men or the encounters.

"Where ... how did you get these?"

"Did you think nobody knows what you do, letting men use your body like that? Do you have no pride? You are Carla Owo. Your name and presence should instil fear and respect, and yet, you reduce yourself to a whore."

Marlon's words stung, and her cheeks burned. She shoved the photos back into the envelope. She'd never felt dirtier about her sex life until now. Until her blood brother called her a whore.

Tears burned the back of her throat, and she was glad for the sunshades covering her eyes.

What right did they have to invade her privacy in this manner and record her sexual encounters?

Anger surged through her, and she turned on Marlon. "Did you do this? Did you take the photos?"

"You think I would've stood there watching your disgusting shows?" He sneered.

"Yes," she snapped. It was precisely the kind of perverted thing Marlon would do.

He shrugged. "I am Marlon Owo. I order other people to do things like that."

"You bastard!"

"Whore!"

"Stop it, both of you!"

Her father's menacing voice drew her attention again.

She sat in the chair, bristling, squeezing her hands together instead of punching Marlon.

Knowing her brother and his mean streak, he would smack her right back. He had no problem with inflicting violence against his kid sister. He'd done it before, slapped her so hard, she'd bitten her tongue and bled.

"Carla, you're missing the point. The photos are here for a reason, as leverage. As you can see from the attached sheet, a judge has signed a warrant authorising your incarceration at the Lori Osa Institution for the Insane based on these photos. All I have to do is sign the form at the bottom, and you'll be carted away."

Her body turned cold. She scrambled the sheet and read the words.

The document was from the court, authorising her to be sectioned for committing lude acts of indecency. She could be locked up in a sanatorium, drugged up and out of her mind, for however long her father wished. No one would come to her rescue.

This was a whole new low.

Her father, the man she called Daddy, was blackmailing her.

People who should love and take care of her—a brother who called her a whore and a father who would lock her up in a mental institution. They had conspired against her.

All this, just so she would do what her father wanted.

Was there any wonder she was screwed up and needed drugs, alcohol and sex to escape it all?

Jaw clenched tight, heart pounding, headache looming, she glared at her father. She didn't think she'd hate her old man and brother more than she did at this moment.

Resentment or not, there was nothing else to say except, "I'll do it. I'll get married to Alhaji Sani's son."

She used to think the day her mother died was the worst day of her life. This was now the worst day of her life.

# NINE

"THERE'S SOMETHING off about this," Duke said, scrolling through the screen of the device in his hand as he assessed the payment cycle and gambling trend for one of their clients.

It had been two weeks since his return from Idunnu Resort. Two weeks of getting back to his job overseeing the Odili family business empire and territory that held over ten million people.

"Mr Ujam has a death wish," Mason said from the driver's seat as they headed out to visit one of the Opal Casinos regulars. "He's already defaulted on his payments by two weeks. And he dared to tell one of the runners he wouldn't be making the payment."

The Odili family was one of the largest families in the Yadili network. Don Sylvester Odili, Duke's uncle, was one of the most powerful men alive.

Yadili was a secret society founded as a vigilante network to protect and progress the region when people of the tribe were being persecuted. Members took an oath of allegiance to a particular way of life and started off as apprentices, working their way up the levels through the years.

The Odilis ran a very tight and clean operation. Their main interests were in finance, and they controlled most of the casinos in the region.

As Yadili, they had sworn to give back forty percent of their income to their communities. Unlike the government, they had created jobs for locals, and given free education to every child, providing community sustainability in the region. The citizens lived a relatively good life, the economy of the area was buoyant.

In a few months, Don Sylvester would announce his heir. Duke was promoted to his position when Alfred Maduka, Mason's father, died. Being underboss didn't automatically make Duke heir, and he didn't take it for granted. There were other potential heirs like Mason and his brother Rocha.

Duke took his responsibilities damned seriously. And now he had to deal with a wealthy client who owed a considerable debt.

"Exactly the reason I think something is off. From the records, he's never missed payments before. He's been able to rack up this high level of playing credit with the casino. And now, he just stopped paying? Is he having problems at the ranch?"

"Nothing that showed up. His bank accounts look buoyant. There's no reason he shouldn't pay his bills."

"Hmmm." It seemed Mr Ujam wanted a visit from Duke.

Usually, there were other people, runners, down the chain who dealt with debt collection. But Ujam was a premium account, a big roller, which warranted notice from Duke himself. So, Mr Ujam's behaviour raised suspicions.

Mason turned the car off the highway down the private road leading to the ranch. Trees lined the unpaved path on both sides, with fields stretching out as far as the eyes could see. Cattle grazed on the left field while pigs roamed in a pen on the right side. Gravel crunched under the tyres as they drove up to the large, country house.

"It's quiet," Mason said when he killed the engine.

"Yes," Duke observed. This was a place usually busy with workers on an activity or the other. But apart from the animals grazing, no humans were visible.

"Stay alert," he said, stepping out of the car. He reached for the pistol and listened for sounds.

Mason rang the doorbell.

Something whizzed past Duke's head. *Thwack.* It embedded into the wooden door.

"Down!" Duke shouted and hit the deck.

Adrenaline kicking in, he rolled over and aimed the gun in the direction of the bullets heading in their path. He fired two shots. A quick glance at Mason showed he was firing shots in the same direction. The only structure that could hide shooters was the barn building. Using hand gestures, he indicated for Mason to head right while he went left.

Not knowing how many people were firing shots made it tricky. But there had to be more than one based on the trajectory and rounds fired. Something glinted in a gap through the wooden structure. Duke took aim and fired. Heard a gasp and a thud. One down.

The one-year military service that every member of the Yadili had to undertake came in handy now.

Mason covered Duke as he ran toward the side of the barn, keeping low as bullets whizzed past him. By the time he got to the front of the building, liquid trickled down his left arm. A quick glance revealed a flesh wound where a bullet had ripped through his triceps.

Adrenaline in his system dulled the pain. Leaning against the wall, he ripped the bottom of the shirt and bound the injury to stop the bleeding. Although he felt no pain, he didn't want to bleed out before he'd gotten to the bottom of this fracas.

Checking his bearing, he sidled down the narrow strip, found the door, kicked it in, and dodged the bullets that flew out.

Mason ran towards him. He stopped on the other side of the entrance and stared at Duke's arm.

Duke shook his head as an indication he was all right. With a left flick, he indicated they were going into the barn.

Mason nodded then counted down from three with his fingers. At one, they both fired shots into the barn as they entered.

Duke hit an assailant on the mezzanine who tumbled and landed in the hay. Mason got the third man hidden behind a stall door.

They checked the area. Three assailants, all dead. None of them was Mr Ujam.

"What the fuck was this about?" Mason kicked one of the dead men, showing his rising anger that a routine debt collection had turned into a bloodbath. Mason was a hothead. He was always likely to act first and ask questions later.

Duke was the opposite.

Mason's eagerness to get to Mr Ujam and deal with him for the unpaid debt had led them down here today into a trap.

"Kicking him won't give us answer," Duke said in a tone that let him know he wasn't pleased, either. "We need to find Ujam."

He nodded, and they went out, eyes and ears sharpened for more surprises, and guns raised. After kicking down the door to the main house, they found Mr Ujam skulking in his study, throwing things into a leather briefcase.

"Going somewhere?" Duke asked in a calm voice.

He jerked, dropping the items he'd been holding. Eyes bulging, he gulped and backed away. "Mr Odili."

"You look surprised to see us, Ujam." Duke strode to one of the sofas and sank into the velvety softness, the gun still in hand and pointing downward. The man was very wealthy, and this room reflected it with expensive furnishings. "Come and sit down."

Sweat dripped down his face, and his hands wrung restlessly as he took faltering steps to the armchair.

"What do you want?" Ujam asked.

Mason strode over, pushed him into the chair, and stood behind him.

"I'm a very reasonable man. But I'm confused this morning. We came here to settle a debt, and instead, we were dealing with an ambush."

His guilt was written all over him as he avoided Duke's gaze and shifted about in the chair.

"Mason, please show Mr Ujam we mean business."

His second grabbed the man's hand and held it against the side table while he pulled out a knife. He positioned it above the man's pinkie finger.

"Please don't do this," Ujam cried, eyes wild.

"For each question left unanswered, Mason will cut off a finger. So, let's start with a simple one. Where are the rest of your family?"

His throat rippled as he swallowed. "My wife took the kids to her sister's."

It was the middle of the holiday season so an entirely plausible explanation. However, Duke suspected there was more.

"What about the farmworkers and domestic staff?"

"I-I gave them some time off. They've been working hard."

"Bullshit," Mason said. "You don't send the whole fucking crew away at the same time."

"It's just you in the ranch today?"

Another gulp and he nodded.

"Who were the three men shooting at us from your barn?"

"I don't know anything about that," he said quickly.

Duke gave the nod. Mason held down the man's hand, lifted the knife, and brought it down with a hard crunch. Mr Ujam gave a long, blood-curdling scream. His last finger rolled onto the table, hacked clean off at the first knuckle. His eyes went back into his head, and he looked like he would pass out.

"Stay with us," Duke said.

Mason tore Ujam's shirt and bound his hand with it. He then smacked the man on the face. Ujam's eyes flew open in a wild and pain-filled expression. Not a good idea for the man to bleed out or pass out before giving them answers.

Duke had no remorse for hurting this man, especially since he was involved in trying to kill

Duke and Mason. Greed had made Ujam risk his life when he could have paid his debt. He'd wanted to avoid them and have other people killed instead.

"If you don't want to lose more fingers, I suggest you start telling the truth. Tell me why men were trying to kill Mason and me on your ranch."

His face became ashen, sweat dripping down his skin. "I—I had a visit from someone who told me I didn't have to pay off the debt if I helped him. He—he said I would get VIP passes and credit to the casinos across the regions. I owed so much already I didn't want to lose the ranch. So, I agreed."

"And what exactly did you have to help him with?"

Grimacing, he averted his gaze. "I was supposed to arrange for you to come to the ranch and leave the rest up to him. He told me to send my family and everyone away. When the men arrived, I knew something bad was going to happen."

"Fuck!" Mason looked murderous.

"Who is this man, and why does he want me dead?"

"He introduced himself as Mr Akindele from Lori Osa."

Duke and Mason looked at each other at the same time. They both remembered that name.

"Mr Ujam, we came here to collect a debt, and we never fail in our mission. Now, for being involved in such a plot, your debt is doubled."

"What? You can't do that," he protested.

"I certainly can. You were stupid enough to think you couldn't pay what you owed, and you made me come out here. Then to top it off, you tried to kill me. You either pay up or be ready to make your family homeless and your wife a widow."

His eyes rolled back, and sweat dripped down his face as he nodded.

"Good." Mason pulled out the tablet and held it in front of him. "Make the transfer now."

With trembling fingers, Mr Ujam typed onto the screen. It took longer since he was obviously in pain and losing blood. The makeshift bandage was soaked red.

"It's done," Ujam said in a low voice.

Mason nodded, and Duke stood. "Get yourself seen by a doctor. You had an accident with one of the farm equipment. You know better than to get the police involved. And while you're at it, see a shrink, too. You have a gambling problem, Mr Ujam."

They left him. Outside, Mason called Maddox, the enforcer, and told him what had happened. Maddox's clean-up crew would get rid of the bodies and identify the attackers. Duke's team would deal with the perpetrators themselves. No police involvement required.

"That name he said in there, Akindele, you recognised it, right?" Mason drew his attention with his question.

"Yes. It's the name of the driver of the car I asked you to check out for me two weeks ago. The one from Lori Osa." The same city that Carla—Carla Owo—lived in. This was too much of a coincidence.

"First, he follows you. Now, he wants to kill you. What's going on?"

Duke exhaled a sigh. "While I was away, I met someone, a young woman. It turned out she was John Bull Owo's daughter. I didn't know until afterwards. Mr Akindele works for him."

"The Baron?"

Duke nodded.

"John Bull is one mean motherfucker, and you fucked his daughter. No wonder he wants you dead." Mason paced, gravel crunching under his shoes.

Crazy thing, Duke wanted to fuck the man's daughter again even knowing what she had done. "I don't give a damn."

Mason leaned against the battered car. "Tell me what happened."

Duke settled next to him and explained how Carla had approached him in the club, Duke's dismissal of her and subsequently saving her in the alley. Taking her back to the hotel and spending the night and the next day with her.

He skimmed the details.

However, Mason would notice the softness of this voice as he spoke about the lady and know how much she had gotten under Duke's skin.

Then his voice hardened as he recalled confronting the men following Carla and her subsequent confession about setting Duke up.

His fury rose again at the memory and her cutting remark to Jide when she was unaware that Duke had returned to the hotel suite.

After she'd left the suite that day, Duke had slapped Jide for the first time since the man started working with him and warned him never to talk to Carla like that ever again. Then he'd ordered the man to pack up their things. They'd left the hotel that afternoon and had flown home by private jet. The items he'd bought for Carla were stashed in a bedroom in his house. He'd planned to give them away to charity but hadn't gotten around to it yet.

"This is fucked up. What are you going to do?" Mason asked, drawing him back to the present.

Carla's father was a rival and had made it known a long time ago that he was their enemy because they had refused to work with him on his drug business. They had cut off all his supply routes into the Odili territories.

Sleeping with his daughter had been unwise. However, The Baron taking out a hit on Duke's life was extreme retaliation. He hadn't coerced Carla or forced himself on her. She had instigated their interaction, and there had been mutual consent through it all.

"I'm not going to wait for the next wave of assassins to come after me," Duke said. "I'm taking the fight to The Baron. I'm going to Lori Osa."

# TEN

"WE LOST the three men sent to Opal City," Marlon Owo announced as he sank into one of the soft, dark brown leather chairs in front of his father's large mahogany desk.

John Bull pulled open a left-side drawer and withdrew a cigar. After inhaling the smooth, aromatic scent, he rolled it between his thumb and fingers before snipping off the round tip. Lighting it, he then leaned back into his armchair and took a puff, allowing the rich cedar smoke to float into the space around him.

"The men were dispensable. If not, I wouldn't have chosen them," he said before taking another puff. "They are just casualties of war. A war that will see our territory expanded."

A war that would put him on top of the cartel hierarchy and make him the most powerful man in the continent. A far cry from the impoverished boy who'd grown up in the slums.

He'd been born to poor, hardworking parents. His family had survived the tragedy of armed massacres. Many people had been forced to live isolated in camps. Over time, the fields had turned into slums characterised by substandard housing and squalor. His father had eventually found low-paid work at the docks, and his mother had done volunteer work helping other low wage families.

John Bull had grown up in the slum. One day, his father had taken him to the docks to show him where he worked. John Bull was supposed to join him there when he became old enough. On the way, they'd travelled in a packed bus filled with sweaty, smelly men. John Bull had noticed the lovely houses, cars, and people dressed in beautiful clothes, unlike any he'd ever seen in the slum. At the docks, he'd noticed the men who'd come from the slums were the ones working hard carrying the bulky goods coming off the ships. The men shouting out orders were the ones who'd arrived in sleek cars and were smartly dressed.

From that day, he'd hated being poor and had decided he would do whatever it took to escape the slums and poverty. By the age of ten, he'd started stealing money from neighbours, and by the age of twelve, he'd been dealing drugs for one of the local gangs. At fourteen, when his father discovered his activities and confronted him about it, he'd held a gun to his father's head and swore he would kill his old man if he ever got into his business again.

That night, he'd packed his bag and left home. He would remember the tear-streaked face of his mother and the angry face of his father. But there was no turning back for him. He'd begun his ascent into power.

With a mix of intimidation and manipulation, he'd risen very quickly in the criminal underworld. He acquired a reputation for being very bloodthirsty and never showed any fear. By the time he was sixteen, he'd committed his first murder and joined the foot soldiers of one of the cartel bosses.

Aiming for the top job, his ambition had no limit.

One day, he would head his own criminal organisation.

One day, he would be the king of the world.

"But Duke Odili is still alive."

Marlon's words drew him out of his reverie.

John Bull met his son's gaze. "Don't worry about Odili. He'll be dead soon."

# ELEVEN

"YOU HAVE a beautiful home," Abdul said as Carla showed him to the pool.

Their parents had arranged this visit so that they could get acquainted before the betrothal got formalised. Last week, she'd gone with Daddy to the Sani's country house in Medogri. This week, Abdul was visiting her without his father.

"Thank you. I thought we could sit out here." She waved at one of the pool chairs. The infinity pool was one of her favourite areas in this house. It overlooked the ocean, and they could sit out here and watch the sunset.

While she had agreed to do this out of coercion, she would make herself as comfortable as possible. Sitting inside was stifling and suffocating. Out here, a sense of freedom swept over her as if she could outrun her problems.

"Good idea." Abdul lowered his body into a chair. He was good-looking and wore a two-piece burgundy tunic suit. His golden watch and neck chain glittered in the sunlight.

If Carla was remotely interested in getting married, Abdul would be a good catch, based on his appearance.

However, his association with her family made him a dismal choice. The last thing she wanted was to marry a man like her father, or even worse, her brother. Although she had no proof of his deviousness, so far.

If she was going to marry him, she needed to figure him out. What kind of man would agree to marry a woman he barely knew?

"So, what do you think about this whole marriage affair?" she asked after she sat on another lounger.

"The whole marriage thing?" His body tensed, and for the first time, he looked annoyed. "Don't you want to get married?"

"Of course not. I'm not ready for marriage, and we're supposed to be married in less than two months."

"What do you mean you're not ready? Twenty-four is old enough, and you're a woman. This is the best time to wed so you can have the children while you're young and fertile."

Carla recoiled like he'd slapped her. He made her sound ancient. "I'm not a baby factory."

He sat up straight, and his eyes darkened. "I didn't say you were. As my wife, you will be the mother of my children."

This guy was turning out to be as terrible as her first instinct indicated. "Don't I get a say? What if I don't want children?"

"Don't be silly." He shook his head as if he really thought she was a silly little girl. "Of course, you want children. Every woman does."

Carla's mouth dropped open, and she stared at him in shock. Ending up in a sanatorium was beginning to sound enticing compared to marrying this misogynistic nightmare of a man. Then again, she lived with two misogynistic men, so what was one more?

"I—"

Sounds of crashing glass and shouting interrupted her, and she turned in the direction of the house.

"What's going on?" Her voice trembled. Her eyes widened.

"Not sure." Abdul rose from the deck chair. "Let me check it out."

"I'm coming too." She shook her head, foot bouncing on the paving stones.

She didn't know what his father allowed in their house, but this was hardly the safest place of Earth. The chance of things going wrong was high. With the quantities of drugs and guns flowing through the home, that likelihood rose every day.

It could be her father having a go at one of his men. Raised voices were a regular occurrence, especially if someone had messed up.

"Okay. Come on." He took her hand, and they walked back into the house.

They descended the short maple stairs from the hall, her heart stopped, and she gasped.

The open-plan sitting room lay bathed with light streaking in from the walls of glass. The usually breath-taking panoramic view of palm trees, cerulean sky, and ocean was overshadowed by the scene of looming violence inside.

In the middle of the space, Triple-D had his left arm wrapped around Marlon's throat, his right hand holding a black handgun to her brother's temple.

She had to blink a few times to make sure she wasn't hallucinating. As part of being on her best behaviour and knowing Abdul was visiting today, she hadn't taken any alcohol or drugs. So, she wasn't high.

From this angle, only his broad back and side was in her line of sight. She recognised the profile. Recalled the feel of his thick hair in her palms, and the unshaven bristles on the chin that scrubbed against her skin as he kissed me, their bodies slick with sweat while he pulsed inside her.

It was Triple-D, all right. Mr Dark, Dangerous, and Decadent himself. Here, in her living room. Looking every bit the powerful man she remembered and sharply dressed in a dark, fitted suit and tie as if he'd just stepped out of a business meeting.

Another man stood beside him, less formally attired in a black t-shirt, navy denim, and black boots, gun raised in Daddy's direction. Father's goons surrounded them in a kind of tense Mexican stand-off.

"Tell your men to back off. Or I'll put a bullet in your son's head." Triple-D sounded calm and authoritative. No trace of fear.

Her limbs shook, and her heart nearly exploded in her chest, it was beating so fast. All because of the number of guns pointed at her ex-lover.

How could Triple-D not be afraid? Didn't he know who he stood against?

A ruthless man, her father wouldn't care about sacrificing his son. He would sooner put a bullet through Marlon himself than lose the upper hand. Perhaps Marlon being the favoured son was the only thing keeping him alive.

Daddy took a cigar out of his pocket, clipped the end off, and lit it as if he had no care in the world. Behind him hung an oil painting of him which dominated the white brick wall.

Whatever reasons her lover from a month ago had for being here with a gun at her brother's head, she needed to do something to defuse the situation. Or there would be a bloodbath.

She would not allow Triple-D to get hurt. Or die.

"Daddy—" She swallowed the lump in her throat. "—Abdul is here."

Abdul held her arm, tugging her to stand beside him.

If a stray bullet hit Abdul, his father won't be happy, and there wouldn't be a wedding. And no alliance. Nothing else was more important to her father's ambition. He needed the expansion into the northern regions.

Heart thumping hard and fast against her ribs, she prayed her father would make the right decision.

In the end, her father waved his hand. His men lowered their weapons and stepped outside.

Daddy sat on one of the white leather sofas, legs stretched out as he puffed on the cigar, his golden Colt 45 on his lap. He collected the damn things and dedicated a room to his gun collection. If it was gold, had bling on it, and was previously owned by a dead drug lord, her father had a cabinet for it.

"No member of the Odili family is welcome here," her old man said. "Unless of course, you've changed your mind about opening up your territories to my shipments."

Wait a minute. Triple-D was a gangster? A man as brutal and deadly as Daddy?

Blood drained from her head, making her body sway. She gripped the edge of a windowsill by the landing to steady herself and not flop on the polished floor like a marionette whose strings had been cut.

"We both know that Hell will freeze first before that happens," Triple-D replied in a deep, harsh voice she barely recognised.

"Then, why are you here?" Dad snapped.

"You issued a hit on my life. I want to know the reason."

No! Carla sucked in a sharp breath and leaned more weight against the ledge.

Why did her father want to kill her ex-lover? Those photos of her sexual encounters flashed through her mind. There hadn't been any glossy images with the two of them in the pile she'd seen. Were there photos of them hidden somewhere in this house?

"I won't waste your time by trying to deny it," Daddy said. "You knew that anything that belongs to me was off-limits to you, yet you chose my daughter. That was an insult to me."

Her father slammed his hand on the tabletop.

Carla flinched at the loud noise, and her shoulders slumped.

This was her fault. She had put a target on Triple-D. If she hadn't manipulated him into sleeping with her, he wouldn't be in trouble with her father.

Holding her breath, she expected the man to spill the beans about what had happened to exonerate himself.

"I take responsibility for my actions," Triple-D said, adding to her shock. He sounded composed, still not breaking sweat. "It was never meant as an insult to you, Baron. But now that you've drawn first blood, I'm obligated to retaliate."

How Triple-D could still stay composed baffled her. The other man with him hadn't said anything either.

Her father's eyes widened. "What do you mean?"

"To ensure that you don't send more assassins after me, I need insurance. I'll take your son as a hostage."

Everyone in the room gasped. For the first time in her life, Carla became jealous of her brother, wishing it was her in Triple-D's grip. Her as his hostage.

Sweat glistened on Daddy's hairline, and he drummed his fingertips on the table in an agitated manner. He wouldn't want to lose his precious son and heir to his empire as a hostage.

"Dad, he can't do this," Marlon protested.

"Yes, he can, son. It's one of the cartel rules. He is entitled to a first blood hostage."

Carla simmered with anger. As usual, Marlon was the one getting the attention. The one everyone wanted.

She wanted to rush over and kneel at Triple-D's feet, begging him to take her prisoner instead.

Yet, another part of her wanted Marlon and Daddy to suffer for all they had put her through. The latter part won, and she tugged her arm, trying to break away from Abdul so she could go to her room.

"Carla, come here."

The command from Triple-D's mouth made her belly flutter. She froze, unsure of what to do.

"No. Don't go," Abdul said, gripping her tight.

Taking a deep breath, she turned toward Triple-D. He hadn't looked at her since the whole thing started. He wasn't looking at her now.

Yet, she felt him in the beating of her heart, in each breath she took. Knew she had to go to him.

She'd thought about him every day since she last saw him.

Now that he was here, she couldn't stop wanting him and would not give up the chance to be with him again in whatever capacity.

"I have to go." She left Abdul, walked down the stairs, across the marble floor and stopped before Triple-D and Marlon.

For the first time this evening, Triple-D's gaze connected with hers.

Her heart thumped hard. The fluttery feeling returned to her stomach, and she clutched her hands tightly together.

His dark eyes were intense, and when he spoke, his voice was devoid of any emotion.

"Carla, you're going to be my hostage."

# TWELVE

ADRENALINE SURGED through Carla, and a dizzy spell went through her.

Triple-D had picked her as his hostage instead of her brother. She was going with him.

An excited scream bubbled and faded when his fierce expression sent another shiver down her spine. No trace here of the man who had made love to her all-night-long weeks ago.

Gulping down the lump in her throat, she nodded. "O—okay."

A part of her hoped her father would object. Would try to protect her. She was his only daughter, and they needed her for the alliance with Alhaji Sani.

No sound came from her old man. She glanced at Daddy, who relaxed into the chair, smoking his cigar.

A gloating sneer crossed her brother's face as if they were in competition for their father's affection and he'd won.

Carla deflated. Her heart shrank, and tears smarted her eyes. She wasn't as important to her family as she'd thought, after all. She was dispensable.

"Go with Mason to the car," Triple-D said. "Wait for me there."

She nodded. Words couldn't get past the boulder lodged in her larynx.

Something like concern flickered in Duke's gaze and was gone quickly, she wondered if she'd read it right. The only person who seemed to care about her fate couldn't be the person who was angry at her for deceiving him. Was that possible? She must have misread his expression.

He nodded in encouragement, a contrast to the man who had issued harsh orders previously.

Carla glanced at the man covering his back he'd called Mason. She nodded again and followed him towards the front door.

None of the other men in the room said anything as she exited—neither Daddy, Marlon nor Abdul.

She glanced at the men one more time, shaking her head, finally convinced that being Triple-D's hostage was a lot better than being Abdul's wife.

How long did he plan to hold her as a prisoner? Hopefully long enough so that the option of marrying Abdul will be off the table.

Even better if she could convince him to let her stay with him long-term so they could explore their relationship to its full extent.

"—you're in the lion's den."

Carla caught the tail end of Marlon's jibe at Triple-D.

She rolled her eyes heavenwards. Wake up, Marlon. There's a new lion in town.

Her brother needed to smell the coffee.

In all the years she'd been alive, she'd never seen anyone capture a member of the family and invade their home. With her father's reputation, no one would dare. Not even police.

Yet, Triple-D had done something no one else had been able to do—take her father unawares. He'd proven he was a lion—fierce and fearless. No doubt who ruled the situation.

Her excitement ramped. The man was freaking irresistible. She still wanted him—on top of her, inside her, surrounding her. Hopefully, he would do a better job at protecting her than the men she was leaving behind.

However, the sight of all the men with weapons on the driveway dampened her arousal.

Triple-D was like Daddy and Marlon. Men who ruled with iron fists and took what they wanted with impunity. They had no qualms about taking the life of another at the least perceived slight.

How could she care about such a man, no matter how great he was in bed?

No. She couldn't care. Didn't care. Her involvement with Triple-D had been about lust, pure and simple.

She would not care about the man beyond what was required to give and receive pleasure. He was a stepping-stone to help her reach her goal of gaining freedom from her family.

Mason opened the door to the back seat of a blacked-out SUV. Another man she didn't recognise sat at the driver's position. He didn't say anything as she climbed in.

Mason stood outside the car at alert, feet planted apart, handgun still in view. Five minutes later, Triple-D walked out of the house. He said something to Mason that Carla didn't hear and got into the back seat with her, his fingers padding across the screen of his phone. Mason sat beside the driver. The car sped down the driveway and through the gates second of a three-vehicle convoy.

Silence reigned. She squirmed in her seat, aware of Triple-D's quiet presence only inches away. This man had stood up to her father and walked away. She was in awe of him. Her skin prickled, and heat washed over her.

He appeared relaxed as he leaned into the soft leather seat. However, his face had bristles indicating he hadn't shaved for days.

"I didn't pack a bag," she said after they'd left her neighbourhood, unsure of what else to say. Everything she owned was in her father's house except for the clothes on her body and the items in her pocket.

"I'll provide what you need. Empty out your pockets," Triple-D said in a monotonous voice. "Give the items to Mason. Sunglasses as well."

Hands shaking, she passed over her phone and the sunshades that had perched on her head and handed them to the guy in the front passenger seat.

He proceeded to dismantle her phone.

"Hey, that's my—"

"No." Triple gripped her chin tight, making her look up at his face. "You are my hostage now, which means you own nothing. You belong to me for as long as I wish and everything currently in your possession is mine. If you want the privilege of using any of the items, you'll have to earn it first. Am I clear?"

"I—I—"

"Am. I. Clear?" His voice was stern and sharp enough to cut glass.

"Yes, S—Sir," her voice trembled.

Who was this man? He was a strict version of the man she had met a month ago. A man she didn't know very well. A stranger all over again.

Somehow, his hardened tone didn't frighten her. Instead, her heart thumped rapidly against her chest, and a thrill of excitement exploded through her. Was she crazy?

An hour later they arrived at the airport. The transfer from the car to the private jet seemed hurried. It made sense to get out of her father's territory as quickly as possible. Mason led her to a seat and instructed me to strap in and stay there. Triple-D sat in a different section farther away, his back to her, chatting with Mason. Not long afterwards, they were airborne.

Why was he sitting so far away from her? Okay, she was here as his hostage, not his lover. Still, she hadn't expected this aloofness from him, as if they were strangers, not people who had known each other intimately.

Pain ripped her gut. It hurt to see him so distant, physically and emotionally. She swallowed hard, covering her face with both hands.

"Excuse me, Miss Owo."

She lifted her head to find a stewardess standing in the aisle next to her.

"Yes," she replied, wondering if she would offer her refreshments since no one had attended to her since they boarded.

"I've been instructed to show you to the bedroom." The woman replied.

A frisson of excitement went through Carla, making her body tremble. Did Triple-D want her in bed? Was he going to fuck her?

With quaking fingers, she unstrapped the seat belt and followed the woman.

Inside the luxury enclosure that housed a bed, the air hostess took a folded sheet of white paper from her pocket and handed it to Carla. "Follow the instructions."

"What?" Carla stared from the paper in her hand, then back at the woman.

"Follow the instructions written on the paper," she said before walking out and closing the door behind her.

Heart racing, Carla unfolded the sheet and read the boldly scrawled words.

*Take your clothes off. Fold them and leave them on the table, shoes under. Stand at the edge of the bed.*

Her mood brightened. Triple-D wanted to have sex. What else could it be?

Remembering her night with him, she stripped off quickly. Once the clothes were on the table and shoes underneath, she stood by the bed and waited, body trembling.

Triple-D was the kind of man she hated. Right?

So why was she excited about having him in a bedroom with her?

# THIRTEEN

"DO YOU know what you're doing?"

Mason asked the question that had been on Duke's mind since he'd ordered Carla into the car at The Baron's estate.

Letting out a sigh, he tipped his head against the backrest and closed his eyes.

After the failed assassination attempt, they had meticulously planned the assault, investigating The Baron's affairs to discover the weaknesses to his security and where to strike.

His children, Marlon and Carla, were investigated too.

Marlon was an integral part of his crime organisation. He worked as the capo in charge of several operations which included human trafficking.

Carla was listed as part of the organisation, and from their surveillance photos, she had attended some meetings. But there was no concrete evidence of her activities either as a foot soldier or capo in the Owo cartel.

Last week, Duke found out John Bull was in negotiations with Alhaji Sani to merge operations and that Carla was going to marry Abdul Sani. At the time, Duke had refused to dwell on the matter, his anger at Carla's deception still raging.

He'd focused on Marlon instead, who was The Baron's weakness. He was the favoured son, the one whose loss would impact the father's operations the most.

Marlon was as ruthless and bloodthirsty as his father and the old man loved him for it. He was also an arrogant sonofabitch who thought nothing could touch him.

The only way to guarantee John Bull called off his hit men was to use his son as leverage. As a result, they had put Marlon under surveillance, learned his routine and struck.

Today, Duke's team had tracked Marlon to the house he used for his liaisons with women, taken down his security team efficiently, and grabbed him while he'd been balls-deep in some woman's ass.

Everything had gone as planned. Duke had dragged a stunned enraged Marlon back to his house to confront his father. Then Carla had walked down those short stairs, and everything had turned upside down inside Duke.

He had become aware of the thumping of his heart, and his hands had itched to touch her. Then he'd seen Abdul standing next to her, holding her hand as if they were intimate.

Carla might as well have cut Duke with a knife.

She'd looked like she had gotten over their night together.

Then again, she had manipulated him into taking her to the hotel. She had said she'd used him. And she was the reason The Baron wanted him dead.

He couldn't trust her.

Nevertheless, not trusting her didn't stop him from wanting Carla. Didn't stop him from wanting to stomp across the room and rip her away from Abdul, right after he'd punched the man for touching her. Didn't stop him from wanting to take her over his knees and spank her ass sore until she begged him to fuck her.

He didn't care that she was Carla Owo and out of bounds to him.

He'd wanted Carla to himself.

So, as he'd stared down at her father, holding Marlon in his grip, he'd decided to swap hostages—take Carla instead of Marlon.

As soon as he'd called Carla over and sent her to the car, he saw the flicker of triumph in Carla's father's cold eyes.

Duke had chosen the wrong hostage. The disposable one.

Duke had shown The Baron his weakness— Carla.

Now, no matter what lay ahead, Duke refused to regret his decision. He would not have been able to walk away from that house, leaving Carla behind.

Opening his eyes, he stared at his best friend and right-hand man.

Mason never questioned his judgement. On the other hand, Duke had never deviated from a plan like he'd done today. Mason's concern was valid.

"You know you put yourself in a weaker position by taking Carla," he said. "Marlon was the more valuable hostage."

More valuable to The Baron but not to Duke.

Duke became breathless and disorientated.

Carla was valuable to him? Yes, he wanted her as much as his next drink of water. But this was just a physical ache. The girl had done something to him that no other lover had been able to do. Her presence soothed his restless soul.

That was it.

His gut tightened. He couldn't entertain anything more.

For one thing, the girl was an Owo, and he was Yadili. The two didn't mix. Strictly forbidden.

Duke ran a double risk. Not only was Carla's father gunning for him. But if his men found out he had a soft spot for Carla, he would have mutiny. His killer could come from his own ranks.

Concern etched on Mason's face. The man had been beside him since they were boys when Duke went to live with Don Sylvester after his parents' death, first as a best friend and now as an adviser. They worked together, played together.

He trusted Mason with his life. Could he trust him with this?

"I know it's not what we planned," Duke said with a shrug, projecting outward calm. "But I went with my instincts, and they've never failed me before."

"Sure." He nodded, seemingly satisfied with the explanation. "What do you want to do now?"

"Double the security. Everyone needs to be on the alert. Also, maintain the surveillance on The Baron and his son. We don't want any surprises."

Carla's father was as likely to rescue her as he was to kill Duke. He couldn't relax yet.

"Sure."

Suddenly, the stress of the last few weeks sat heavily on Duke's shoulders, threatening to crush him.

Only one person would give him respite like she'd done weeks ago. Carla.

He needed to see her. Needed to touch her, if only briefly. Just enough to quieten the agitation in his spirit.

Could she do it again?

"I'm going to see how the hostage is doing," Duke said as he unclipped his seat belt.

Carla was currently in the bedroom where she'd been ordered to stay. They had another hour before landing. Plenty of time for Duke to get what he needed out of her.

He strode down the aisle. At the door, he took a deep breath before twisting the handle.

Any breath he had in his lungs rushed out at the sight of the naked female form standing at the foot of the bed.

Clothed or otherwise, the woman always took his breath away.

She had flawless dark brown skin on a curvy body, curly hair dangling around her face, and eyes as amber as brandy.

Desire flared in his veins. Damn.

Duke needed to touch her. To taste her. He needed her. Period.

"Triple-D—" she started.

"Don't call me that," he interrupted, partly annoyed about his continued attraction to her. The name had sounded amusing when she'd used in during their night together.

There was nothing fun about this encounter, and he would not let her get the better of him again.

"My father said you were an Odili, but I don't know your name," she said in a soft voice, her gaze on the carpeted floor between them probably from shame because she didn't know his name.

The mix of shyness and boldness she displayed was disarming. She'd used it to play him before, and he'd fallen for it. Not again.

"My name is Duke Odili. Turn around," he ordered in a gruff voice, reaching into a drawer to withdraw the scanner wand. Glad for the distraction so he would not look at her.

She did a slow spin. Her body was unmarred and balanced—boobs fit for his palms, the dip at the waist and then the slope of full hips and rounded buttocks, extending down thighs and legs he pictured wrapped around his hips—perfection, front and back, including the tattoo of a thorny rose on her ankle.

To control his libido, he watched the digital reading on the scanner until it flashed green, giving all clear. No tracking chips embedded in Carla's body.

The scanner had been a precaution.

The government embedded identification microchips in the dermis of the citizens, which could also act as tracking devices and would send signals about the persons' locations.

The wealthy and the elite paid to opt out of using the ID tags.

Carla was in the wealthy bracket.

She shivered. Was she cold?

Duke pulled out a white shirt from another drawer which stored his spare clothes. "Put this on. It'll be big, but it'll keep you warm until we reach our destination."

She stared at the shirt and then at him, a confused frown on her face. "You want me to put it on?"

"Yes, you were trembling. You need to cover up."

"But you left instructions for me to take my clothes off and I thought..."

"You thought I told you to get undressed so we could fuck?"

He'd purposefully instructed her to undress. Firstly, to see her reaction. Secondly, because he'd needed to scan her. But mostly because he needed to keep her guessing, to keep her unbalanced until he figured her out. Until he achieved his purpose.

She did not respond.

"Answer me."

"Yes. Look, it doesn't matter." She turned away and reached for her clothes on the table, rejecting the one in his hand.

Damn her. His jaw clenched and tension built on his temples.

"Don't touch those clothes." His voice was hard and cold.

She stopped, turned to face him, hands akimbo. "Why not? I might as well put them back on."

She had some nerve. Soon he would send her tumbling from her high horse.

He shoved the shirt at her. "I told you, in the car, you don't have any possessions. You take what I give you, or you stay naked."

Her mouth dropped open. "But—but…"

He ignored her as he picked her discarded clothes and stuffed them into a paper bag. Then he opened the door and tossed the bag out. "Maddox, get rid of this."

He shut the door and faced her again, arms crossed over his chest.

She recovered her voice. "What are they going to do with my clothes?"

"Burn them, throw them away, I really don't care. But you're not going to see them again."

"I really like that dress," she whined.

"I don't care." He shrugged.

"Bastard."

"I've been called worse."

She growled and stomped her feet. "If you didn't bring me here for sex, why didn't you just take Marlon? Why the Hell am I here?"

"Well, Miss Owo." He took a step in her direction, his voice low. "Remember the last time we met, you told me that you always get what you want." He lowered his head, ensuring he didn't make body contact and whispered in her ear. "Guess what, I always get what I want too."

She jerked back; eyes widened with shock. "What do you mean?"

He enjoyed seeing the surprised expression on her face. She'd started this game. He could play the game too.

He curled his lips in a smile that didn't reach his eyes. "I wanted you, Carla. So, I took you. Now, I'm going to use you like the hostage you are."

Her mouth dropped open on shock.

He throbbed with arousal, and he imagined sliding his dick in to fill the gap.

Not yet. The time for pleasures would come soon enough.

# FOURTEEN

WHEN DUKE threw out Carla's clothes, tension shifted the air.

Fine hairs on Carla's neck stood erect.

He strode to her, hands in his pockets. Then he leaned in and spoke, his hot breath skittering along the sensitive skin under her ear. "I wanted you, Carla. So, I took you..."

Duke used Carla's words against her. Actually used the same phrase she'd spewed at him the day he'd found out her identity in his hotel room. Except he'd substituted fuck boy for hostage.

Shit.

She'd said those words in anger as a deflection for the things Jide had said and the fact Duke wouldn't forgive her. While she would never go out of her way to cause pain to others when they hurt her, she retaliated. It was a survival mechanism. Lessons she had learned from her brother and father.

She hadn't meant those mean words.

Yet it seemed Duke had taken them to heart.

What now? Did he really intend to keep her as a hostage instead of a lover?

He stood close enough for his familiar masculine scent to fill her nostrils. His hands shoved in his pocket, feet apart as he scrutinised her.

There must be a devil on her shoulder, emboldening her, so she didn't shrink away under his scrutiny or rush to put his shirt on. What other purpose did she have for not putting the shirt on, except to get his attention? To make him lose his control and to turn him on.

Still, he hadn't touched her, and she was naked. Not even when he'd chucked his shirt at her.

The back of her throat hurt, and she broke eye contact staring at the white shirt in her hands.

He really didn't want her. Not like she needed. He'd only brought her here as a pawn in the feud between him and her father.

A feud that she had triggered.

If she hadn't deceived Duke, they wouldn't be in this position.

She understood the cartel rules well enough. Duke deserved a hostage for what her father had done or tried to do. And the fact that he could walk into their home and take a hostage was an even more significant blow for her father.

Daddy had taken prisoners before, and he never treated them well.

Duke didn't have to be kind to her.

This was her fault.

Her hands fell to her side, and she stared at her feet while her belly knotted.

"I'm sorry," she said in a small voice, past the lump in her larynx.

"Look at me," his voice was stern but not harsh. Not threatening.

He never raised his voice. But he managed to convey authority.

There was something about this man that made her want to comply with whatever he said. Heat rushed to her centre, and if she'd been wearing knickers, they would be damp.

She looked up, met his intense black eyes. She swallowed as nervous energy coursed through her, mixing with regret.

"What are you apologising for?" he asked, his gaze piercing, searching, looking beyond her physiology into her soul like he really saw her.

Her stomach was back in knots, and she fiddled with the button of his shirt. "I'm sorry about what I did the other night. I'm sorry for not telling you who I was from the start. I'm sorry for being the reason Daddy wants you dead. I never meant for that to happen. I promise you."

"You want me to believe that you didn't set me up to be killed? That you were not working on your father's orders?" His voice was harsh and cold, his eyes hard like granite.

"No!" Her stomach dropped, curdled. "No. I never wanted you to get hurt. I didn't even know Daddy would find out about us."

"If you didn't do it for your father, why did you do it? You manipulated me into believing those men were going to hurt you, Carla. I could've killed them. Do you have any idea how fucking twisted that was?"

His eyes were boring into her, stripping away her defences, demanding answers.

He would find out her desperate she'd been. She'd done things to get attention from a man who wasn't her father or brother.

Her stomach heaved, and she clutched it, averting her gaze.

"No. You don't look away from me." He gripped her chin tight, making her look up at his face. "If you want my forgiveness, I demand to know the truth."

"I know." She squeezed her eyes tight, not wanting to see the disgust on his face when he found out the truth. "I was desperate, okay? You happy?"

"No. I'm not." His tone was quiet, almost understanding, but still implacable. She couldn't detect any repulsion in his tone. "Open your eyes."

Her first impulse was to obey. Her reservations superseded by the quiet confidence in his manner and an instinctual reassurance he knew what he was doing and everything would be okay.

Her eyelashes fluttered open.

His gaze had the reassurance, still probing but not aggressive. Just observing. "What did you want so desperately?"

She steeled her body and her mind, preparing for his rejection. His condemnation.

"You. I wanted you. I go to Arufin to escape my life, to chase thrills. When you arrived at the VIP lounge, my friends and I saw you, and they bet me that I wouldn't be able to get you. I hate losing bets. So, when you turned me down, I bribed my bodyguards to play along to the deception."

"That was all so you could win a bet." It was more a statement than a question, the tension heavy between them.

"I'm sorry." She grabbed his arms, anxiety coursing through her again that he wouldn't forgive her. He'd been compassionate previously. This situation had turned him into a stranger. She wanted the man she'd spent the night with by any means possible. The man who had shown her more affection than any other man in her life. "I'll do anything you want. Just forgive me, please."

He puffed out a sigh and gripped her chin, his callused fingers rough on her soft skin. "Anything?"

"Yes. I don't want to keep feeling this shitty for what I did."

He stepped away, undid the cufflinks on his shirt and placed them on top of the drawer.

Her heart skipped a beat and started racing as she thought he would take his clothes off.

Instead, he rolled his sleeves up to his elbows, showing off muscular arms. Then he lowered his body onto the edge off the bed. "Come here," he said and patted his thigh. "Lie across my lap face down."

Her heart raced, thumping against her ribs. She wanted contact with him. But he confused her.

"What?" her voice was shaky.

"If you want my forgiveness, your penance will be ten smacks of my hand on your bottom," he said in a matter of fact tone.

A sizzle went down Carla's spine at being spread across his lap, her need for body contact with him almost overwhelming. But smacks? "I'm not a child."

"I'm well aware of your age, Carla." He rubbed a knuckle between his eyebrows and sighed again. Was he tired? The whole thing must be getting to him.

Another wave of remorse hit her. He was a marked man. Marked for death by her father. Because of her.

What were a few smacks on the bum compared to a bullet in the chest?

Her legs shook, her knees weakened from the thought of him hurt. Uncertain about why she was filled with fear for his safety. She wobbled forward and dropped the shirt.

He caught her and held onto her waist. Rough fingers gripped her chin, making her meet his gaze.

"Be sure you want this. Once you get on my lap, there is no going back," he spoke with a deep rumble.

Throat clogged, she nodded.

"I want words."

She swallowed. "Yes. I want this."

They might as well get it over and done. Hopefully, she would stop feeling guilty.

"Okay." He guided her as she leaned over him, her belly and hips on his hard thighs while she braced her hands on the carpet.

Being upside-down made her dizzy, and her heart raced at the body contact.

He swept the mass of curly hair she'd pinned back away from her nape down her left shoulder.

She summoned all her willpower to resist but eventually succumbed. Licking her dry lips, her body relaxed.

His clean earthy masculine essence surrounded her, stirring something deep within her.

Everything else seemed far away as she focused on taking one deep breath after another.

His fingers travelled in a slow trail from neck to bum. Each scrape, each graze sent tingles along her nerve endings.

Her body responded. Her breast growing heavy while the nipples became achy. Liquid pooled between her thighs.

The anticipation and sensation all combined to leave her body covered in sweat and Goosebumps.

His fingers trailed down the crease of her ass and hovered there for a few seconds.

Delicious ache built in her core and she spread her thighs, hoping he would help her relieve it.

His amused chuckle filled the room and her cheeks heated at her lewd behaviour. She clamped her thighs together again.

"Tut, tut, tut," he murmured in disapproval.

Dammit. He had her so overwhelmed, so confused she didn't know what she was doing any more.

She relaxed again, letting her thighs fall open.

"That's better," he said.

The approval was like an injection of pure joy in her veins. A reward she didn't know she needed until now. A stimulant in her brain.

She remembered the night of exhilarating, wild sex they'd had together which seemed like a lifetime ago considering what had happened since.

A finger slid underneath and caressed the smooth skin of her inner thigh.

Her breath locked in her throat, blood whooshing in her ears in awareness and anticipation. She squirmed, wanting to scream for more, deeper contact.

As if in response to her thoughts, he moved his hand higher between her legs and brushed the strip of curls covering her pussy. The almost non-existent caress set her alight with need, making her inner muscles clench. She dripped, coated in wetness.

No way he wouldn't notice how much she burned for him, how turned on she was.

Stomach muscles hardened against her side. He inhaled deeply, the sound of his lungs expanding above the sound of the rushing blood in her ears.

He brushed her clit. She couldn't hold back her moan any more than she could stop breathing. Her body tingled everywhere.

She stiffened her arms, trying to prepare her body and mind for what was to come.

He moved his hand, trailing deliberate, perfect circles around her labia and clit, teasing and driving her insane.

"You're so wet, Carla," he said. He swiped his fingers coated in her juices across her lips, and she tasted her essence. "Is this for me?"

"Yes." The word felt torn from her soul. She braced herself, holding her breath and lifted her head. She was wet because of him. Thrilled about joining the mile-high club while his men were outside the thin partition.

He withdrew his fingers and licked them, a wicked grin on his face. "I'd almost forgotten how fucking sweet you are."

He teased and tortured her, making her squirm and moan. Before she could scream her frustration, he thrust fingers inside her wet channel, fucking her with his digits one moment and changing the angle in another and grazing her sweet spot.

She cried out, her skin crackling with sensation, pleasure fizzing in her veins. Lost in the rising euphoria, she gripped his legs for anchor, ready to fly.

His fingers left her body. Shocked, she gasped for air. "Oh—"

His palm cracked across her bum in a resounding thud.

"Shit." She jolted, almost bolting away from his body.

He clamped her with the one arm, while the other came down on her body in hard swats. No matter how much she wriggled and tried to get away, she couldn't. Yet she didn't tell him to stop.

A strange exhilaration burst through her veins like when she'd had a sniff of blow. A delicious naughty sensation took over her body. She welcomed every crack on her heated bottom, sending her closer and closer to release.

Her nails dug into the muscles of his legs.

He didn't seem to mind. He returned his fingers inside her, thrusting in and out while still slapping her bum, the sounds of her wetness joining the smacking noise.

"Oh … oh … oh…" She climbed towards bliss when his fingers curled and grazed her sweet spot again and again.

Her climax hit her like a high-speed train, knocking her breath out and tearing a scream from her lungs. Waves and waves of pleasure crashed over her making her tremble.

The intensity was too much. She started sobbing, tears running down her face.

Duke withdrew his fingers and sat her upright, caging her in the cocoon of his arms and body as she rippled with wonderful aftershocks. She snuggled into his warmth and gripped his shirt while her tears wet his chest.

Gradually, her body stopped shuddering, and she became aware of her surroundings. The unmistakable evidence of his erection strained the fabric of his trousers and prodded her bum cheeks.

What she would give to have his hardness inside her.

He leaned back and tilted her chin up. "Do you feel better?"

"Yes," she replied. She felt warm and pliant, not ready for this encounter to end. "I'm sorry about ruining your shirt."

She swiped at the black mascara streaks, although she liked to see her mark on his shirt. It identified him as hers, if only for now.

He grinned, the first she'd seen a proper grin on his face today. "Don't worry about the shirt. The past is forgiven."

A smile bloomed on her face. She'd almost forgotten how gorgeous he looked when he smiled.

"Do you mean it?" She sounded childlike in her joy.

"Yes. I want you to understand that no matter what goes on with the business or the world generally, when it's just the two of us, I will always take care of you. But you always must tell me the truth. Can you do that?"

"The truth. That's all you want?" Her face puckered as she scrutinised him. This man kept surprising her.

"It's important to me that you never try to deceive me again," he said, his expression serious.

Considering he'd forgiven her previous actions, making this promise seem like an easy option. "Okay. I promise, Duke." Carla rolled his name around her tongue. It sounded good.

Their gazes locked, tension building between them, making her breathless.

"Are you going to marry Abdul Sani?"

His questions caught her off-guard, and her stomach knotted.

First instinct was to deny it. However, she'd just made a promise, same as she'd promised her father.

She swallowed a few times before she got her tongue to work. "Yes. The wedding is all planned for a few weeks. Daddy and his father are in business together."

He stroked a finger down the side of her face and nodded. "Your father should call off the hit in a few days, and you can go home."

"Really?" She searched his face, not sure if he was joking.

Duke never said things he didn't mean.

He nodded and switched her to sit on the bed. He stood and shoved his hands in his trouser pockets, distancing himself, his expression guarded.

"Once your father calls off the hit, I have no reason to keep you. Put the shirt on. We'll be landing soon."

He swivelled, grabbed his cufflinks from the dresser and walked out of the room.

Carla sat on the bed for a moment, in a daze.

Duke's words should fill her with joy at the idea of going home soon.

Yet her stomach rolled, and her chest felt weighted with dread.

# FIFTEEN

"Take your seats and prepare for landing," the captain's announcement came through invisible speakers.

"Oh, no." Carla pushed off the bed and picked Duke's shirt she'd abandoned on the floor. Pulling the buttoned-up clothing over her head, she shoved arms into the long sleeves. The cotton fabric fit, skimming her curves and chaffing her nipples, the length almost to mid-thigh.

A look in the narrow mirror above the vanity showed it didn't look too bad. A wide belt would turn the outfit into a fashionable boyfriend shirtdress if only she had one.

Without undies or shoes, the outfit was the least of her problems. Duke had taken everything else, and she wouldn't stoop to wearing his boxer-briefs or footwear or whatever else he had in the lockers.

Tap. Tap.

Carla swivelled at the sound. "Who is it?"

The door slid sideways, and the stewardess who'd attended to her previously stood there with a pair of double-plait, toe-thong, tan leather sandals in her hand. "Mr Odili wants you to have these."

"Whose are they?" Carla took the clean, polished items. However, the scuffs beneath the heels showed they'd been worn.

"They are mine. Mr Odili requested a pair of shoes for you. These are the only spares I have in my cabin bag."

"Oh. Thanks. But I can't take your stuff."

"It's okay. He has already paid more than they're worth. So, you can have them."

"Thank you." They were little more than flip-flops, and not to Carla's style. But beggars, and all.

Obviously, Duke hadn't planned for her presence. Hence the lack of alternative clothing when hers had been taken. Still, his improvisation was sufficient, and the problem was solved.

"You need to take your seat and put your seatbelt on," the woman said, waiting beyond the threshold.

"I'm coming." Carla glanced at her reflection once more, using fingers to detangle and tidy the mass of curls falling around her face. She shoved her feet into the flat shoes, followed the air hostess into the aisle and halted.

In the first bank of four cream leather seats, the men were in conversation. The private jet had one chair on either side of the narrow aisle with reasonable gaps between opposing chairs for legroom and the collapsible lacquered tables used for dining or working. On the left side, Maddox—she assumed—faced her. Duke was adjacent on the right side while Mason sat opposite, back to her.

Duke lifted his head. Black eyes ringed with heavy lashes stared at her, piercing straight to her soul.

Her heart skipped a beat. Her knees jellied. She gripped the top of the empty seat to her left.

Blinking, he looked away, his attention back on whatever Mason was saying in a low tone. His middle finger rubbed back and forth over his lips.

Only minutes ago, his hand had been on her bum setting her skin ablaze, and inside her fuelling her climax. Could he still smell and taste her essence?

As if he read her thought, his pink tongue flicked out and swiped the pad of his long finger. He might as well have swiped his tongue on her clit.

Desire flared in her veins. Her core clenched. Suppressing a moan, she closed her eyes, clamping her thighs together.

"Ms Owo."

Carla's lashes fluttered open at the sound of her name. "Yes?"

Four pairs of eyes were on her—the three men who had stopped talking and the air hostess pointing at an empty chair in the next section.

"Take your seat."

Had she moaned loud enough to attract attention? She would just die if she had.

Laughter lines crinkled Duke's eyes and his mouth tugged up at the corner in slow amusement.

Her cheeks heated. She hurried and tumbled into the first chair without any elegance. Her bum ached from the spanking, but she was glad the men couldn't see her.

Still aroused, her pulse raced, her breathing irregular and shallow. At this rate, there would be a wet patch on the shirt since she had no knickers to absorb the moisture slicking her thighs.

Why did the man get her easily excited? He knew how to push her button.

She strapped on her seatbelt and squeezed her eyes shut, trying to take calming breaths. Otherwise, she would walk down the aisle, sit on Duke's lap and ride his dick, the rest of his team be damned.

With her eyes closed, Duke filled her mind. Her chest tightened.

How could she remain attracted to him knowing what she knew about him?

He was a ruthless and dangerous man, no different from her father and brother. She hated men like her father, didn't she? Why didn't she hate Duke? Shouldn't she hate him more now because he'd taken her as a hostage?

Despite the incongruous connection they had, she trusted him more than she trusted any member of her family. She couldn't wipe the memory of how he'd taken care of her the first night they'd met.

"…when it's just the two of us, I will always take care of you…"

He'd said those words after he'd spanked her and given her the best orgasm yet, made her ache and soothed the pain in the most delightful way.

She believed him. He followed through on his vows.

A bump made her opened her eyes and look out of the window. In the fading light of dusk, the plane landed and taxied along the runway towards the terminal building. The airport seemed to be in the middle of a city, but she couldn't recognise it. The plane stopped, and three large blacked-out SUVs pulled up close. The seatbelt signed went out.

Carla glanced in Duke's direction. He unclipped his seatbelt, stood and looked at her. With a small nod in her direction, he walked out.

Mason approached her. "Come with me."

"Okay." She undid the harness and followed him out. Descending the stairs, she caught a glimpse of Duke as he got into one of the cars.

Mason ushered her into the backseat of a different car and got in beside her.

Why wasn't she in the same car as Duke? Strange, she missed having him beside her in the backseat even if he wasn't talking to her.

Mason was handsome, but he wasn't Duke. He chatted with the driver in Igbo, and she didn't understand what they talked about.

Not that she paid attention. Clasping hands on her lap, she looked out the blacked-out windows. The dusk light made it difficult to make out much of the location. Buildings, traffic jams, and pedestrians. It seemed like some other cities in the country she'd visited. Although tempted to ask Mason where they were, she didn't. When he wasn't talking to the driver, he was engrossed with tapping on his handheld-device.

Tall orange lamps lit the winding road on the hillside. Sparse houses scattered around the valley of the suburban location. They pulled into a gated property surrounded by a high-security fence and stopped behind the first car.

Mason got out and held the door for her. "Come on."

She stepped out onto the portico held up by two white columns in front of what looked like a magnificent mansion. Security lights lit the driveway. There were at least five cars she could see mostly SUVs and one sportscar. Activity bustled around her. Men unloaded items from the just arrived vehicles.

Mason ushered her into the luxurious house with a modern open space design of white walls and natural tone furniture and furnishings, paintings on the wall and sculptures on plinths. They walked up the grand staircase and turned right on the landing. No one else came into view. She was mesmerised by the beauty of the space.

"This is your room," Mason said, holding the door of a bedroom open. "You're not allowed out of here unless you're told to do so."

"Um, what if I need the bathroom?" She looked around the simple room. It seemed out of place in the house considering the luxury just outside the door. A low bed covered in white sheets and pillows, not much else. No drawers or table. A simple light bulb in a cone shade suspended from the ceiling.

"You can use the one through that door." He pointed at another partially closed door.

She walked over and pushed it, revealing a wet room with a shower unit, a water closet, a white sink and an empty cabinet above it. A plastic cup on the sink held an unopened toothbrush and toothpaste tube. A black towel hung on a chrome rail.

This room was more clinical than the bedroom.

She left the bathroom and shook her head.

Mason had gone, the bedroom door shut.

Did he really mean she couldn't leave this room?

She tested the door. Yep. It was locked, and the window was barricaded with metal bars.

Shit.

Where was Duke? Why hadn't she seen him since they'd disembarked from the plane? Would he come to see her later?

Heart racing, her mouth dried out. She rubbed hands over her face in an agitated manner. The white walls combined with the lack of tasteful furnishing was freaking her out, reminding her of another place.

A place she didn't want to go.

She flopped in the bed, taking huge gulps of air to calm down.

No need to panic. This was Duke's house. He wouldn't leave her alone for too long. He would come to see her as soon as he could.

Standing in front of the mirror in the bathroom, she plaited her hair into four rows to save it from tangling and shrinking. Afterwards, she stripped off and took a shower. The warm water beating on her skin helped to soothe her mind and body. Feeling sleepy, she climbed into bed naked, the sheets cool against her skin. The combination of the quiet humming of the air conditioner and cold air lulled her to sleep.

Carla woke to the sound of birds chirping. Soft sunlight streaked through the parting in the blinds.

Nothing else gave an indication of time. No clock. No phone.

She rolled out of the mattress and walked into the en-suite. She brushed her teeth, turned on the faucet and went under the shower. Her stomach rumbled. She hadn't eaten anything since lunch with Abdul in her house. Was that only yesterday? It seemed more like a week ago.

Out of the shower, towel around her body, she realised she didn't have a change of clothes.

She put the shirt back on, opened the door, stepped out and froze.

A dark-skinned man she didn't recognise stood in the room, dressed in a button-down blue shirt on dark denim and black shoes. With a crew-cut, he looked older than Jide but younger than Duke or Mason. He held a smirk on his face as he sized her up.

"Who are you?" Her voice sounded squeaky, and she hated it.

Hated that the presence of another human being could leave her jittery. Hated that she didn't know when she would see Duke? Hated that he wasn't here right now.

"My name is Emmanuel," he said and lifted the tray in his hand. "I brought your breakfast."

Couldn't he have knocked before entering the room?

"Put it on the bed," she snapped.

There was no other furniture available.

He ignored her instruction and raised his brow. "It seems you have no manners. I should go and come back when you get some."

He moved towards the door.

Dammit. Hungry and not knowing how long before the next meal arrived, she relented. "No. Sorry. I didn't mean to be rude."

He stopped but didn't turn around. "You have to beg me o."

She rolled her eyes heavenwards.

The consequence of being a hostage—any Tom, Dick or Harry felt they could insult her. Her father's status as a rich and powerful man meant nothing to these people.

Since she wasn't in a relationship with Duke, they didn't care, which kinda infuriated her because she would label Duke as her boyfriend, in a heartbeat.

She sucked in a harsh breath at the realisation. She wanted to date Duke. An impossibility under the current circumstances.

Puffing out air, her shoulders slumped. "Emmanuel, please can I have the food?"

Turning around, he had a triumphant smirk on his face. "Of course, you can."

He pushed the tray in her direction. When she reached for it, his hands brushed hers.

She pulled back, shocked at his audacity. "What are you doing?"

"Nothing. Just passing you the tray." He leaned against the wall.

She frowned, stiffening her spine and tilting her chin up. "Thank you. You can go."

"No. I have to wait for you to finish eating so I can take the tray back."

Did they think she would steal the cutlery or something?

She huffed, sat on the bed with the tray on her lap and opened the covered dishes. The smell of the fried plantain and scrambled eggs got her salivating. She ate the food like the hungry woman she was and drank the coffee too.

She forgot Emmanuel was there until he asked, "Have you finished?"

"Yes," she said and passed him the tray. "Thank you."

"You're welcome." He headed for the door.

"Can I ask something?" she spoke up as he turned the handle.

"Sure." He looked over his shoulder.

"Is it possible to get some fresh clothes? I've only got a shirt."

"I'll speak to Boss about it and see what he says."

"Thank you."

He nodded, tugged the door open.

She managed a quick glance into the corridor before the quiet thud of the frame blocked the view and Emmanuel was gone.

***

Later that first afternoon, the items Duke had bought for her on Pleasure Island were delivered to the room—clothes, shoes, purses, accessories, everything. They were still in the shopping totes and got stacked in a corner.

There was no TV or phone or tablet to distract her. That night, to stop from thinking about being locked up in a white room with barricaded windows, she played dress-up, trying on the different outfits.

If only Duke was there to watch her dress up. Then she would strip them off in a tease, and they would make love afterwards. Maybe an opportunity would come later for her to try them on again.

However, the third night's sleep was fitful. The nightmare about her mother's death haunted her. She woke in a cold sweat, shivering while her waking mind replayed the scene over and over, Mummy at the bottom of the stairs, blood everywhere.

When Emmanuel brought breakfast, she hadn't showered. He didn't say anything about her dishevelled state. Not that she cared about his opinion. She picked at the meal, barely tasting the fried beanballs.

"Don't you like akara?" he asked.

She shrugged and lifted the tray towards him. "I'm not hungry. You can take the tray."

He pushed off the wall and took the item. "Are you okay?"

"I'm not okay. Where is Duke? Why hasn't he come to see me?"

Emmanuel chuckled. "You mean Boss? Boss wey don travel."

Carla jerked back as if he'd slapped her. "Duke travelled? When? Where to?"

"It's none of your business. The only business you have with the boss is as his hostage."

Carla's skin overheated and her breaths came in short pants. Nausea churned her stomach.

Duke had travelled without informing her. No word. Nothing.

How long was she supposed to stay locked up in this room? With nothing but four white walls, a pile of clothes and nightmares for company.

Desperation clawed at her skin. Her hands shook.

She couldn't spend another day in this room. "Emmanuel, you've got to help me."

"What do you want?" He tilted his head to look at her.

"Can you get me out of this room?" She was ready to do just about anything to get outside.

He did a full belly chuckle. "Of course not. You want the boss to kill me?"

She pushed off the bed, stomping her feet as she paced. Her mind whirring with alternatives. Maybe going outside was impossible. There was a risk someone else would see her.

"Okay. Forget that. Can you get me some blow or weed? Just something to get me through the days, eh. I'm going out of my mind in here." She waved her arms in agitation.

"You really want some blow?" he asked in a surprised voice.

"Yes, do you have some?" Her heart rate picked up. If he was asking, then it was a possibility.

"Not on me. Boss doesn't allow any of that shit in this house. But I can get it."

"Yes, please. When can you bring it?" Hope flared in her veins, and she wrapped her arms around her midriff to hide their trembling. She could wait a few hours to escape from her mind.

"I have to talk to a guy who knows a guy." He winked. "But if I bring it, I want something in return."

"I don't have money to pay for it." The bags in the corner caught her attention. "But I have some expensive clothes you can sell. They are designer and unused."

"Nah. That's not going to work."

"What then?" She rocked in place, despair threatening to overwhelm her.

He glanced at the door, came close and lowered his voice. "My deal is when I bring the blow, you let me fuck you."

"What the fuck? No." She shrank back from him, her stomach heaving.

She wasn't attracted to him. And there was the thing with Duke. She couldn't imagine any other man touching her in that way. Although Duke was a bastard for keeping her locked up and going on a trip.

"Then, no deal. Good luck with being stuck in here for weeks while Boss is abroad." He walked to the door.

"Wait!" Carla panicked and clutched her head. Pain exploded in her chest, her mind whirring with white noise. It had only been a few days, and she was almost climbing the walls and clawing at her skin. She had to do what she needed to keep sane. "Okay. We have a deal. Can you bring it tonight?"

The triumphant smirk was back on his face. "Sure. I'll see you later."

***

"Get up!"

The loud shout had Carla jumping out of bed to face two huge men in the room with bleary eyes. These hard-muscled guys were covered in t-shirts, denim, and tattoos.

Heart hammering in her chest, her gaze darted from the tall one to the shorter one, their expressions icy. For the first time since she arrived here, she felt threatened like something terrible would happen to her.

She must have fallen asleep while waiting for Emmanuel to bring her dinner and the stuff she'd ordered.

She took a step backwards, bumping into the wall before she noticed Jide step around the men.

"Wh—what's going on?" she stammered, her voice a little shrill, throat dry.

"Sorry." Jide shrugged noncommittally.

The men ignored her and started dismantling the bed.

"Jide, what's going on? Why are they doing this?" she braced arms across the midriff, glad to be in denim shorts and a tank top.

"The boss ordered it. You've lost your privileges," Jide replied.

Privileges. That word again. Duke had mentioned it in the car the day she arrived.

"Why?" she asked.

Jide nodded toward a corner of the room. She peered at the round reflective object she'd assumed was a light bulb. He tugged her arm and dragged her into the bathroom.

"Look. You shouldn't have told Emmanuel to get you some blow," he said in a low voice.

"What? How do you know?" Her face heated up.

"The camera records everything that goes on in this room. Boss streams it on his device. He's not happy. This is your punishment."

"Omigod!" She covered her face. She hadn't realised there was a camera in the room. "Do they all know what happened?" She indicated the men currently in the bedroom carting away the last furniture. Where was she supposed to sleep now?

Jide nodded.

Shit. She gripped her head and paced the bathroom. Everything was going wrong. This wasn't what she'd hoped for when she'd wanted to be Duke's hostage. She hadn't expected to be treated like an actual hostage. Now, she was being punished. What next?

"So, this is the naughty girl."

Carla whirled around at the new voice and noticed a woman standing at the bathroom entrance. She had long, jet-black hair that reached her waist. Tall, slender body in black leather corset, leather trousers, and stilettos and cheekbones on a face for a cover model.

"Jide, you can leave us," the newcomer continued. Her voice was vibrant and sultry.

Jide backed away, giving Carla an apologetic grimace.

"Turn around," the woman said.

Indignant, Carla stood still, staring at this person she'd never seen before, wondering what she wanted with her.

"I can see what Duke means. You need to adjust your attitude, don't you, Carla?" The woman sighed. "Does your father ever take hostages?"

Carla swallowed the lump in her throat before answering. "Yes."

"Then you know what comes next and how you should behave."

Carla had never paid much attention to her father's prisoners. The ones that lived were kept in little more than cages. They were brutalised if they disobeyed orders. Her father was not a kind man.

Was Duke the same?

She glanced at the men who now stood at attention in the bedroom as if awaiting their next order. Would he permit these men to mistreat her?

Her stomach knotted, and her throat became sore. The boldness deserted her, and she realised she wasn't brave enough to push her luck.

All the woman had asked her to do was to turn around. What harm could come from that?

She nodded before shuffling three-sixty degrees.

"Good girl," the woman said when Carla faced her again, a smile curling the corners of her lips. "My name is Madam Sophie. I'm in charge of the brothels, and you are now my responsibility."

"Duke would never let me work in a brothel!" Carla screeched in outrage. This had to be a bluff, probably to scare her into compliance.

"Since you decided to transact your body for goods. It is only fair that Duke gets his percentage entitlement. So, he's formalising the arrangements."

"Oh, no. Tell me he didn't hear that." Carla felt sick, and she clutched her belly. She hadn't thought anyone would overhear the conversation, let alone Duke.

What must he think of her? She hadn't even thought about what she would do when Emmanuel arrived with the blow. She'd been going out of her mind and not thinking straight.

"Oh, he heard every word of you offering your body to one of his men. Gentlemen, please take her down to the dungeon."

Sophie stepped out of the way, and the two burly men approached her.

Shit. Her recklessness had landed her in hot water. Again

"No. Listen, I didn't mean it. I wasn't going to sleep with Emmanuel!" Carla screeched in protest as they carried her out one on each arm, her feet not touching the floor.

No one paid any attention to her words.

# SIXTEEN

AT TEN at night, the door to a local bookie in the south side of Opal City was kicked in. Wood splintered against the brick wall and glass shattered into tiny fragments onto the floor.

The four men around a table in the back room sprang from their seats, scrambling for their items. The hefty man who stood guard pulled his gun out of his holster, and opened the door leading to the corridor.

Pius, the manager of the betting shop who was also the dealer tonight, quickly cleared the table of the cards in case it was the authorities who'd arrived unannounced. Gambling wasn't illegal, but there were restrictions on the type of gaming as well as the times, including the level of high stakes on the table tonight.

Pius quickly hid the cards and chips in the secret compartments. The last game would have to be voided. In the five years since he'd been working here, they'd never been raided by law enforcement. In fact, he knew of a few policemen who frequented the establishment after hours.

This shop was owned by Rocha Maduka, one of Duke Odili's capos, and Mason Maduka's brother, and an inducted Yadili. He was untouchable as far as law enforcement was concerned, so whoever had ordered this raid, if this was what it was, was asking for trouble.

Crack. Crack. The sound of gunshots filled the enclosed space, and the men stiffened. Quickly, he ushered them toward the back entrance. Before they could escape, three men with metal pipes and guns blocked their path.

Pius didn't recognise any of the men.

"What the fuck," he shouted, perhaps unwisely.

In response, one of them rushed at Pius and smashed him into the wall, the rod in his hand digging into his throat and almost cutting out his breathing. With one man pointing his gun at the gamblers, the other went about smashing every item in the room with the makeshift weapons until splinters and shards showered the linoleum flooring.

When they were done, the men stared at him with icy gazes that made fear slither down his spine.

"This is just a warning. This is now our fucking territory. If you want to keep doing business here, you have to start paying protection money to us."

"What? We've never needed to pay money before. This shop is in Don Odili's territory."

"Well, times have changed. The Baron has come to town, and you can thank Duke Odili for making it possible."

"What do you mean by that?"

In response, the man pulled back and smashed Pius's side with the pipe, sending him careening into the corner as pain seared down his body.

All the men laughed, and a few minutes later, they were gone. The gamblers didn't stay to help Pius either, and he had to drag himself off the floor in search of Uba, the doorman. He found the man in the reception area, with blood splattered across the white walls and floor. He placed a couple of fingers at the base of his throat to check for a pulse but got none.

Exhausted, Pius leaned on a chair, pulled out his phone, and made a call.

# SEVENTEEN

DUKE SAT in the den discussing business with his four capos. The beam of sunlight from the bay windows turned the cigarettes' smoke into a white haze floating across the room.

Only an hour ago, he had returned from a week-long business trip abroad. He'd barely had time to walk through the front door of his Opal City home before he'd headed into an emergency meeting convened because some of their businesses had been hit by thugs sent by John Bull Owo. No significant damage had been done, but one of Rocha's crew had been shot and lay seriously ill in the hospital.

"We can't let them get away with this," Rocha Maduka spoke, his voice thick with arrogance and annoyance. He was Mason's hot-headed older brother.

Duke understood Rocha's response. He wanted to retaliate, and send men to destroy property and threaten lives, which in turn would be a declaration of all-out war between the Owo and Odili families.

There hadn't been major hostilities involving the Odili family for a generation. With the inception of the Yadili network, they had opted to collaborate and cooperate where possible and split territories along family lines. Duke didn't want to be the man to break the peace.

He could be as ruthless as his enemy, showing no mercy when necessary.

Still, there were other ways of resolving this without shedding too much blood. Only the person with the best strategy would win the war.

The men argued back and forth. There seemed to be a 50-50 split.

Duke sat there watching them, listening to their debate. Ultimately he would make the final decision on what needed to be done.

"Mason, what do you think?" he asked, always keen to get his best friend's opinion on matters like this. They didn't always agree on everything. But Mason was more objective than the rest.

"I don't think we should rush into anything. The Baron has always wanted one thing. For us to open our territories for his drug traffic. We need to let him know it is not going to happen."

"Perhaps we should let the drugs in," Charles said. He oversaw their sports and events betting and worked closely with Rocha. "We spend so much time and effort policing our turfs. For each drug dealer we get rid of, two more take his place."

"Exactly," Rocha butted in. "Not to mention the income we're missing out on."

"That's not how we do business here," Mason replied. "We all took an oath when we became Yadili. We all swore to no drugs."

"But times are changing and think about all the money. We cannot be beholden to rules set by our fathers which are stopping us from progressing. Others are raking in cash. Why shouldn't we?"

"Rocha, we all make enough money," Duke spoke up. The time had come to bring the meeting to order and to a conclusion. "We don't need to dabble in the toxic substances. It is hard enough to keep our streets clean as it is without flooding it with The Baron's cocaine or meth. We make enough to keep our families and us in lavish lifestyles for generations. And that is because we have a tight grasp of our territory. We won't let John Bull spoil things for us. Increase the security on all the businesses for now. Neutralizing the Baron is my responsibility, and I will get it done. Whatever I decide, I will talk it over with Don Sylvester first before we implement. Are we on the same page?"

The men murmured their agreements.

"Good. Let me know what resources you need to get the shops up and running again." Duke met Rocha's gaze. He was the one most affected by the recent attacks.

"Yes. Will do," Rocha replied, his annoyance seemingly defused.

Duke shifted in his seat. "You know I've just got in from a long flight. So, if there's no other matter—"

"There is one more thing. We haven't seen the hostage yet," Rocha interrupted him.

Duke stiffened. He'd tried to keep Carla out of his mind for the past few days. Not since the bullshit incident between her and Emmanuel in her room.

At the time, Duke's fury had bordered on catastrophic. He'd wanted to cancel his trip, board a plane straight back home and cut out the hearts of the motherfucker and the bitch and feed them to the pigs on his farm.

Mason had talked him down from the ledge. He'd ordered for both Emmanuel and Carla to be locked up separately in their secure facility until he returned and put Sophie in charge of minding Carla. It seemed his men couldn't keep their dicks in their pants while he was away. He'd switch off the live stream from the cameras around Carla. No one had been allowed to remind him of the girl.

Until he was ready to deal with her.

He had to deal with her. Carla had disrespected him in front of his men. Not to mention Emmanuel, who was already suffering.

Duke had to maintain the status quo. No one could disrespect him and get away with it. No one.

Not even Carla.

There was a price to pay.

Now Duke took a shallow breath and released it, keeping his rage at bay. "I believe she's with Sophie."

Rocha grinned. "Oh, this I want to see. John Bull's mafia princess in chains."

Duke's scalp prickled. He wanted time to deal with Carla privately. The capos were entitled to see and assure themselves she was treated appropriately...like a hostage.

Anything else would be misconstrued. As far as they were concerned, the daughter of an enemy was an enemy. And they were probably right. Especially now that John Bull had sent men to attack Odili businesses. His capos wanted their pound of flesh. And Carla was it.

"Of course. Let's go to the dungeon."

The men followed Duke.

The house was built in a villa-style with quarters running North, East, South, West all linked by corridors. The underground space was a mix of a car park on the west, gymnasium and indoor swimming pool to the south, with the cells to the east. The cells were rarely used. Occasionally, they were employed to house prisoners who needed questioning.

Carla was the only hostage he'd had for a while. Duke had assigned her a room in the main house instead of one of the cells. He'd corrected that mistake. Since she chose to betray his trust, she had to live with the consequence.

They walked into the dungeon, which consisted of stripped-back brick walls and a concrete floor. Brick and metal separated the units.

In one of them, Carla dangled from chains hooked to a pulley system, arms and legs splayed wide, dressed in a black lace bodysuit which was no more revealing than some swimsuits.

Damn. No matter how fucking pissed off Duke was at her, she still made his dick stand up and take notice on sight. She was becoming his addiction. No doubt about it.

Sophie stood next to Carla, talking in a low voice. Carla's head hung forward, the brown curly tresses obscuring her face.

Did she know he was in here?

Duke stepped into the cell, unable to keep his distance.

Sophie looked up, her eyes widening briefly. "Gentlemen, what brings you down here?"

"I wanted to see how you were doing with the hostage," Duke answered as he strode towards Carla.

Her body stiffened, and the chains rattled as if in response to his voice. She didn't lift her head, though.

A fizz of pleasure went through him, and he tamped down the urge to praise her. They were a long way from compliments.

"She was very raw to start with, but she's a quick learner," Sophie replied.

"Good," Rocha said as he strode to the wall with the rack of tools and picked up a vibrator, weighing it in his hand. "I'd like to see a demonstration."

Duke clenched his fists, his back muscles tightening.

Rocha was beginning to piss him off, walking around the place like he was calling the shots.

Mason leaned against the metal bars near the door with his arms crossed over his chest, his gaze seemingly more intent on Sophie than Carla. Charles stood by the opposite wall, rubbing his hands as if expecting a show to start while Maddox hadn't crossed the threshold, legs spread apart arms across the chest.

"She's not ready for a demonstration," Sophie said, eyeing the men. "Maybe another day or two."

"She is a prisoner, isn't she? She takes what's coming to her."

Rocha was testing Duke's authority, trying to find out if he had a soft spot for their captive. Any show of affection would put him in a weak state. Any of these men wanted to be in his position. They were sharks, and if they smelled blood, Duke was a dead man.

Sophie looked at Duke, her eyebrow raised, seeking his permission. Sophie understood the politics of the situation.

Duke hated being put in this position, especially by a woman. A woman who had no respect for him.

"There will be no fucking demonstration until I say so. Maddox, bring Emmanuel in here." Duke ordered, reasserting his authority.

"Sure." Maddox moved out of view.

Rocha grumbled something he couldn't hear.

Duke ignored him and went over to Carla. With a hand under her chin, he lifted her head until she stared at him, eyes sparkled with defiance. The bratty princess still lurked inside.

Duke hid his smile. The devil in him would enjoy taming the hellion.

First, he had to deal with business, then he would get to the personal stuff.

Rattling chains announced a new arrival.

Duke swivelled as Maddox pushed a groaning Emmanuel to his knees. The man's clothes were torn and caked in blood, his face puffed up and bruised from the beatings he'd received the last few days.

Duke had no sympathy for the man who had disobeyed his strict rules about drug usage in his house, not to mention his inappropriate proposition to Carla.

"Maddox, strap him to the bench, face up." Duke stretched out his hand without looking at his second. "Mason, give me your knife."

"Please, don't do this." Emmanuel struggled as Maddox lifted him.

Duke held onto Carla's neck to keep her head up so she could watch the proceedings. Her eyes widened, the pulse at the base of her neck thumped fast and hard.

Mason placed the item into his hand, and the metal caught the light.

Carla's breath hitched.

"Oh God," she cried.

He pointed the knife at Emmanuel. "This is what happens when you incite my men to disobey me."

"Please—"

"Shut up." His grip on her neck tightened, his anger surging. "I don't want to hear your voice. I don't want to hear a word from you. Keep your eyes open and watch."

She clamped her mouth shut and nodded.

He released her and stalked over to the bench. Emmanuel was secure with cuffs around his ankles and wrist and connected to chains bolted into the concrete floor. His head dangled off the edge of the bench backwards. He shifted in obvious discomfort as Duke approached.

"Boss, pl—"

"Pleading is not going to help you." Duke pressed the tip of the blade against the man's throat.

Emmanuel's Adam's apple bobbed as he swallowed.

"Good. I'm going to ask the questions, and I need honest answers. Or I'm going to cut your tongue out."

Carla gasped and started panting loudly.

Duke didn't turn to face her. If he did, he might not complete his actions. And he needed to finish this to show these men that he was still in charge here.

"Did you know that I banned everyone from consuming drugs in my house?" Duke asked.

The man swallowed. "Yes."

"So why would you disobey my rule and bring cocaine into my house?"

"I'm sorry, sir. She asked me to get her some."

"By 'she' you mean Carla?"

"Yes, sir."

"And who is she to you?"

"Nobody, sir. She's nobody."

"So, you flaunted my rules for a nobody."

Emmanuel whimpered.

Duke depressed the sharp blade deep enough to nick the skin. Blood welled up from the small gash. "You better give me a fucking answer."

He whimpered again. "It was the Devil, sir."

Duke laughed without humour. "Haven't we heard that before. You mean the Devil got into your head or was it your trousers and forced you into asking your boss's hostage for sex? Because that's the reason you brought blow into my house, right?"

"Yes, Sir."

"That's okay, then. Maddox, release him."

Duke passed the knife to Mason, who wiped it with a cloth and placed it in the sheath attached to his belt.

The enforcer stepped forwards, unchained the bound man, and helped him rise.

Emmanuel stood, facing Duke.

"This is the last time I want to see you at my house."

"Please, boss. I won't ever do it again."

"That's good because if you tried, you'd be dead. Now get out of here before I change my mind."

Head bowed, Emmanuel hobbled out of the cell.

Duke met the gazes of his capos. They all stood still, watching, waiting for what he would do next.

Slowly, he turned around, unable to avoid the inevitable.

Carla had set them on this course, the moment she told Emmanuel to acquire drugs for her, especially with the complication of her father attacking their business premises.

"Sophie, bring the whip," he said, walking over to Carla.

"Now we're talking," Rocha commented. "I want no mercy. I want to see her blood streak all over her back just as her father's men spilled Uba's blood."

Carla's eyes glassed over, and her lips trembled. "Pl—"

"Shhh." Duke pressed his fingers to her lips as he gripped her chin. "Don't say it."

That humane side of him that she seemed to reach into stirred and made him want to send everyone else away so he could spend time with her in here, punishing her, pleasuring her. He pictured bending her over the bench and fucking her until they were both boneless.

Instead, he leaned in, so his mouth brushed her ear and whispered. "You're going to be brave and take your punishment. For me. For us."

He'd survived this long, and his men respected him because of his fairness. He wasn't cruel. There always had to be balance. He couldn't punish Emmanuel without punishing her. She'd been the instigator, the more serious offender.

If she hadn't asked for blow, none of this would have happened. He would have been able to shield her from the 'pound of flesh' demand from his men.

Her eyes glimmered with tears. She swallowed and said in a low voice. "I'll do it, for you, for us."

He cupped her nape and her face. The way she looked at him, they could have been the only two people in the dungeon.

"Don't ever disrespect me in front of my men again," he said quietly.

"I won't. I promise." Her voice was firm and resolute.

He brushed his lips against her ear and whispered as he caressed the other cheek, "Good girl."

He stepped away and said to Sophie. "Five strikes. Keep the strokes to the back only. I want no marks on her front. Also, no criss-crosses on the skin."

"Yes, Boss," Sophie said.

He walked to the door and swivelled to face the men. "No one else is allowed to touch her," he said while meeting their gazes one to one.

They nodded.

He walked out, the zipping whip resounding in his mind.

He entered his private living room, shut the door, and turned on the music. The sound of an aria from the opera drowned out any sounds possibly coming from Carla.

He couldn't have stayed to watch her bleed any more than he could have whipped her himself. He got no sick pleasure from seeing people hurt. He just wasn't built that way, no matter how many times he'd had to do it.

At a time when he was vulnerable to her father's attacks, he didn't want to deal with a mutiny from his men as well. They would kill her if they felt she would jeopardise their business. And they would kill him too

Duke paced the room, refilling the brandy glass each time he stopped at the bar. He hadn't felt this jittery since he'd been a boy dealing with the death of his parents. He didn't understand why he was so rattled. There should be no reason for him to feel this way. He'd tortured others, even killed before.

So why should this one be different?

Carla deserved punishment. Her father wanted him dead, and Carla was the reason.

"Fuck. Fuck. *Fuck!*" He threw the glass, and it smashed against the wall, sending brandy and shards all over the marble floor.

The phone buzzed. He pulled it out of his pocket, tapped and raised it up to his ear.

"It's done," Sophie said on the other end.

Duke strode to the window and glanced out.

His capos were getting in their cars, Rocha and Charles laughing.

"Bring her to my room," Duke said.

"It's not a good idea, especially in the middle of her training," Sophie replied.

"If I wanted your opinion, I'll ask for it. Just do as I said," he snapped.

"Of course." She sounded offended.

Duke ignored her and switched off the phone. This wasn't the time to allow anyone to question his actions. The capos were doing that already. He strode to the landing and waited.

A few minutes later, Jide climbed the stairs, carrying a limp Carla over his shoulders, followed by Sophie.

Duke opened the bedroom door and pointed at the massive bed in the middle of the room.

"Place her face down," Sophie instructed.

Jide obeyed, putting Carla on the comforter.

Carla didn't stir, though.

"What happened?" Duke asked, concern rising.

"She passed out," Sophie replied. "I've cleaned out the wound and applied the healing salve."

She put a bottle on the bedside cabinet. "She'll be good as new in a couple of days."

"Thank you," Duke said.

She nodded and walked out of the room, taking Jide with her.

As soon as the door closed, Duke strode to the bed and knelt beside it, hand cupping Carla's cheek. Her skin felt warm. She shivered and moaned softly.

Duke kicked off shoes, climbed in and scooped her on top of him.

After a while, she stirred and nuzzled his neck.

"I did it," she said in a low voice.

"You did very well, Carla," Duke replied, throat thick, eyes smarting.

"Anything for you. For us," she whispered. "There is an us, isn't there?"

Duke's heart clutched tight. Was it just delirium from the pain, or did she really mean it?

"Do you want an us?" He wasn't sure about anything with her. She continued to confuse him. He wanted a relationship with her, didn't he?

Her hand on his arm tightened. "Yes, please. Let's start afresh. Just you and me."

For a moment, he couldn't speak as the band in his chest tightened again. When he spoke, his voice was husky with unexpected emotion. "Okay. We'll start afresh. Just you and me."

She fell asleep, the sound of her soft snore filling his room.

Duke lay there with her for a few minutes. He had to do something to stop a war with Carla's father. He would not let her be a sacrifice next time his men wanted a hostage.

He moved Carla slowly until she lay on the bed and covered her with a sheet. Then he returned to his lounge to make a call.

# EIGHTEEN

CARLA WALKED out of the bathroom attached to Duke's bedroom, covered in a robe.

It was the first time in days she'd managed to take a proper shower.

She had spent nights barely sleeping on a cot not large enough for one person in a concrete and metal cell. During the day, Madam Sophie trained her as a pleasure therapist.

She'd made jokes about selling her body if she needed money.

However, the reality of learning all the different ways she would have to please a client had scared her to death. If she ended up as one of the workers in Madam Sophie's brothels, she would lose the ability to choose her sexual partners.

She shivered, stepping out of Duke's room, and walked down the corridor towards the old room.. Although she had been sleeping in Duke's bed since his return from his business trip, her clothes were still in there.

Thankfully, her time with Sophie was over. The woman wasn't mean, but she was strict. The way she wielded a riding crop like a pro and would flick it on any part of Carla anatomy when Carla misbehaved hadn't prepared her for the sharp sting of the whip though.

That had hurt like hell. Carla had screamed and fainted after the fifth lash.

Waking up in Duke's bed had been the ultimate reward.

For two days she'd been cooped up in his room while the welts from the whip healed. The cream he applied on her skin daily helped to dull the pain. On the first day, he and Jide had installed a TV inside the room so she would have entertainment while he worked. He had brought her meals up to her and had helped her clean up. And for those two days, he had been working from home instead of going out.

Duke hadn't been in the room when she'd woken this morning. Feeling no pain, she'd gotten out of bed and had gone in the shower.

A smile curled her lips as she rummaged through the clothes hung up in a row, trying to decide what to wear.

Duke was a complex man. An enigma.

The past two days he'd been attentive and affectionate, making sure she was comfortable, providing anything she asked for, taking care of her like a lover would although there hadn't been any sexual contact between them since on the flight here a fortnight ago.

And yet, he was the same man who had ordered for her to be whipped by Sophie. Without mercy. Although she heard his remorse when he'd climbed into bed with her and scooped her up after the whipping.

Yet, she wasn't angry at him. Conflicted? Yes. But not angry.

Duke's ability to inflict pain, even indirectly, on another person marked him out as someone like her father.

However, would her father be this compassionate to a woman who was his hostage?

Perhaps if he was sleeping with her too.

Her heart rammed in her chest, and her hand froze on a dress.

Was that all she was to Duke? A fuck toy? Someone to keep his bed warm.

Her father would never invite a woman to his home or to his bed. He modus operandi was to visit his various mistresses for an hour here or there and return home to sleep in his own bed.

Duke had kept Carla in his bed for days and hadn't once tried to get in her panties.

He had similar attributes to her father. But he wasn't The Baron.

Duke was Duke. And he'd promised to give their relationship, whatever this was, a second chance, which she wanted more than anything else.

She grabbed a dress—a short, belted multi-coloured silk caftan that reached mid-thigh. She'd had enough of Duke playing the gentleman.

She was ready for him.

Sitting on the stool in front of the dresser, she creamed her body and put on black lace underwear before tugging the dress on. She finger-combed out her hair, applying the gel that helped curl definition. Then she found some pop socks and wore a pair of black ankle boots.

Dressed, she sashayed out in search of Duke. This was the first time she walked freely through his home.

The place was huge. The corridor on the top floor had rooms on one side and balustrade running along the four balconies which overlooked a lobby below. The ceiling sloped onto a glass skylight in the middle, which also had a chandelier suspended from it.

There were three doors on the side she stood, which meant there were three rooms on the other side as well making six rooms at least on this level. The walls were pale smoke and the doors frost in colour.

Laughter and conversation drew her attention, and she walked to the metal balustrade. Jide and the two men who had dragged her to the dungeon two weeks ago sat on chairs in the foyer below.

Jide looked up and saw her before she could move away from the edge.

"Hey," he said. "Do you need anything?"

"I was just looking for Duke. Do you know where he is?" she asked.

"If you come down, I'll take you to him."

"Okay." She walked along the landing until she reached the stairwell which concealed the steps.

Jide stood when she entered the lobby. One of the men said something in Igbo she couldn't understand. The other made what sounded like a rude sound in his throat. They all gawped at her as if they saw her for the first time.

Her spine stiffened.

Granted, the men might not like her very much. She'd gotten one of them beaten and fired. They had justification.

However, the past two weeks of her life felt like two years. She was a different person now. Not the petulant girl who had arrived here two weeks ago nor the scared girl in the dungeon.

She'd learned from her mistakes and had grown some.

Now, she was dating a mafia prince. She needed to embrace being a mafia princess. She had to act the part if she was going to earn the respect of these men.

She had to do it for Duke. For them. She wanted to stay here. To be with him, feud with her father or not. She didn't want to go back home to her father and Abdul Sani. No. Not Abdul.

So, this was going to be her new home. She had to start getting along with these people so they could stop seeing her as the enemy.

"Jide, please introduce me to your colleagues," she said, hands clasped together in front of her, keeping her poise neither haughty nor submissive. Just confident enough to be taken seriously. Her stint in a finishing school for young ladies, coming in handy.

Jide jerked back in shock but recovered quickly. "This is Fabian—" he indicated the one on his left first and then the one on his right "—and this is Lebechi."

"It's nice to meet you, gentlemen, formally." She nodded at them. "Now, Jide, please take me to Duke."

"This way," Jide said, a grin splitting his face.

The two men still had shocked expressions when she walked away. Good.

"You're really something," Jide said when they were out of earshot of the men.

Carla shrugged. "That's good to know. At least it put a smile on your face."

She hoped it meant he would become an ally.

"It sure did." He stopped in front of a door and tapped three times.

"Jide, come in," Duke's voice came through the panel.

Carla gasped. "How did he know it was you?"

Jide chuckled. "Boss can explain it to you if he wants."

He twisted the handle and pushed the door, holding it for her to walk through.

Carla entered the modern office. Bookshelves lined the right-hand wall, windows on the back wall and an L-shaped desk with several monitors on it stacked against the left wall.

Duke lifted his head from the screen on the desktop and his brow wrinkled. "Carla, you're up. Is everything okay?"

"Of course, I feel perfectly well." She walked to the desk and leaned her hip against it, not wanting to go one hundred percent when there was someone else in the room.

"But your back—"

"—is healed. No need for me to spend another day in bed. I thought you might be able to spare thirty minutes and have lunch with me."

She turned her attention to the other man in the room. Mason.

"Interesting." Mason stared from her to Duke. He stood, seemingly taking the hint. "I'm going to head off. Enjoy your lunch."

"I'll call you later." Duke also got off his chair and came around the desk as the door shut behind his capo. "I told you to take it easy for the rest of the week."

"I'm not very good at obeying orders, remember?" She fluttered her lashes, trying to play at angelic as she took the step to bridge the gap between them.

He chuckled and cupped her cheek, making her skin tingle. His face lit up, and his eyes sparkled, reminding her of the man she'd fallen in love with over a month ago.

Her heart drummed fast in her chest. She was in love with Duke.

Was he in love with her?

"I know that too well. But you shouldn't interrupt me when I'm in a meeting," he said, the amusement taking the sting out of his words.

"Oh, was that important?" She did the innocent girl act again, stepping away from him. "I guess I should go then. You probably don't want to know what I was going to offer you for lunch."

"Now, you have to tell me." He leaned against his desk and crossed legs at the ankles.

"If you want to know, you're going to have to catch me first," she teased, ready to bolt.

# NINETEEN

"IT'S LIKE that, huh?" Duke asked, still amused.

Although he didn't move from the desk, Carla's heart raced with excitement. His gleaming eyes showed his interest.

"Yes, it is." She took another small step. She didn't exactly want to expend too much energy in a race when there were pleasurable alternatives. But she loved pulling out his playful side. He knew how to put her at ease, how to make her laugh out loud. "I'm not an easy girl, you know."

His chuckle was so hearty, the warmest rumble she'd ever heard from a man. It was blissful and erotic all at the same time. "Easy is not a word I'd use to describe you, Cara."

She paused, tilted her head. "You called me Cara again. Getting a little confused, are you?"

She yelped as he sprang forward in a fluid, catlike motion. She didn't have enough time to bolt before he clamped her shoulders in his hands.

His right palm slid up to her neck, cupping it while he lowered his head and whispered. "I'm not confused, Cara. It means darling or dear or beloved."

"You addressed me with an endearment on the first night we met? Wow." She stared at him in amazement. To think she could have lost this man because of recklessness and selfishness.

"You had an endearment for me as well, didn't you? Wasn't it a lingerie size?" He winked at her.

Her cheeks heated. She giggled. Before she could respond, he tugged her neck and lowered his head. Her breath caught in her throat as his lips covered hers.

His tongue glided over the seams of her mouth. She let out a soft moan, opening for him as she latched onto his shoulders to keep steady. His kiss was gentle and slow, with just the right amount of pressure, making her nipples harden with excitement. He kissed her as if he savoured her, as if he treasured her, deeply, thoroughly.

He lifted his head, placing soft pecks on the corners of her mouth.

"I'm in love with you," Carla said, unable to contain herself. She wasn't one to hide emotions, and there was no better time to tell him how she felt.

Duke pulled back, and a frown creased his brows. "You expect me to believe that? You've barely been in this house for two weeks, and you were locked up for most of it. We haven't spent that much time together. How can you be in love with me?"

He stepped away, staring at her as if she was an alien.

Her heart clutched tight. This wasn't exactly the response she'd expected from him. She'd expected some shock but not rejection which hurt the most.

"You know what?" She stalked towards him and jabbed her finger on his chest. "I'm tired of being treated as if my opinion doesn't matter. Daddy and Marlon do it all the time. Even Abdul Sani was already telling me what he expected from my body as his wife—" Duke stiffened, and his hands turned into fists when she mentioned Abdul's name. But she didn't stop and turned away from Duke, heading to the door. "—you of all people were the last person I expected to treat me in the same manner. But I should have known you would be exactly like Abdul."

Duke grabbed her shoulders and spun her around, his eyes blazing with irritation. "Don't you dare compare me with Abdul Sani. I'm not like him."

"Oh, you don't like it? Now you know what it feels like when you tell me I don't know what I feel." Old habits kicked in, making her defensive enough to throw words like grenades like she always did.

Her heart felt like it would punch a hole through her chest. Her hands trembled at her sides, her palms clammy.

He stood so close; his breath fanned her face. His eyes were as dark as the sky at midnight and as intense as the sun on a hot summer's day.

"You're playing with fire," he warned. Something wild flickered in his gaze.

"Then set me ablaze," she dared him. Her mission was still to make him insane with wanting her.

The air in the room seemed to have been sucked out. Her throat locked tight as she tried to swallow.

Hungry for his kiss, she went onto her toes and closed the gap between them until her lips brushed his.

A growling sound filled the room before his lips crushed hers. The kiss was punishing and passionate as tongues clashed. Her arms around his body, her hands clawing at his shirt as she whimpered for more. He fisted her hair, tilting her head to deepen the kiss.

Damn. This man was intoxicating. Addictive. She rubbed her body against his, the hard points of her nipples squashed between their bodies.

He released her and stared down with softened eyes. "You are such a brat, you know that?"

She nodded, feeling a little triumphant. "Works for me as long as I'm *your* brat."

He chuckled low. "You've always been mine."

"Then do both of us a favour. Fuck me."

He whirled her and shoved her face down on the desk, gripping her hands behind her. His free hand stroked her hip and tugged her dress until a pool of silk settled around her waist, baring her bottom to his view.

"Fuck." He growled the word. "You make me so hard."

His words were like a power drug fuelling her body. She'd never had a lover who made her feel as bold and confident as he made her feel. Her sex throbbed, and she ached for him.

The evidence of his arousal nudged her hip. His finger skimmed the thin thong fabric showing off her ass now covered in her juices as she clenched over and over.

"Hold on to the desk and spread your legs for me," his voice was husky as if he could barely control himself.

She did as he wanted, opening herself for him.

His fingers tugged the thong aside. She glanced back to find him kneeling with his head between her thighs.

First, he inhaled deeply, his face rapt in bliss, eyes closed.

"Oh God," she moaned. He hadn't touched her, and her orgasm was imminent.

He ran his hands down the back of her thighs, and then his fingers grazed her pussy lips, circling her clit before thrusting fingers inside her. "Do you like this?"

"Yes," she said, barely getting the word out as she clenched.

He swore again, slowly taking his digits out and sliding them back in. He kept pumping her while his tongue circled her clit.

She couldn't control the movement of her hips as she rocked to his rhythm. Between his fingers working her and his mouth sucking her, she saw stars. Her breathing became choppy, and her climax rushed at her before she could hold back.

She flopped on the desk in a haze trying to catch her breath. The sound of his zipper had her glancing back.

"Tell me how you want me." He lifted the foil of condom with one hand while stroking his shaft with the other, the rest of him still covered in clothes.

"I want you. No barriers." They'd discussed and used protection during their one-night stand. They'd been strangers then. Now, she was all in or nothing.

Tossing the pack, he lined his crown up with her slit and rammed his thick dick into her wet channel.

"Aah," she moaned and gripped the table edge tighter, his size and pressure all too much at once.

"You want me, don't you?" He stilled, his voice an uncertain rasp signalling his control was slipping.

"Yes, I want you so damn much," she moaned and pushed her bum to grind onto his groin. "Don't stop."

She wanted him like this—unrestrained. Everyone else saw the dominant man but no one else say him uncontrolled. No one else saw him vulnerable. Only her.

"Then take me." He pulled out. Leaving only the broad tip to breach her channel. "Take all of me."

His tone was heavy. He meant more than his physical self.

Duke was offering his entire being—the good, the bad and the downright scary. She couldn't pick and choose which parts of him she wanted and which sections to throw out.

He held still, waiting, his muscles bunched, fingers gripping her hips.

She braced on her elbows and turned her head to look at his face with only one reply on her mind. "Yes, I want all of you. Don't hold back."

He slammed into her, the intensity of his gaze making her heart catch in her throat. Pleasure and pain swirled around her, heating her skin. Her toes curled inside her boots.

With each of his thrusts, her hips jerked, her body sliding over the desk. Each back-and-forth motion emptied her out only to fill her up again.

He grabbed a fist full of her hair, making her body arch, deepening the angle of contact.

Her pleasure rose, and she moaned over and over as she rocked her hips. "Oh…oh…oh."

"You're mine now," he said in a guttural tone. "No one else should ever see you like this. Nobody else should ever touch you like this. Do you hear me?"

There was menace in his voice as if he would cause harm to anyone who touched her.

Still, she welcomed his words. She was made for this. Made for him. "That means you're mine too."

"Yes. I'm all yours. Take all of me." He kept slamming in an out of her.

The rush of hormones and sensation was heady as she edged towards another climax.

"Duke?" she could barely say his name, panting.

"Yes?" his reply was more of a groan. He tugged her hair, lifting her head up.

"I'm going to come."

"You wait for me." Leaning over her, he covered her body with his and kissed her, his mouth claiming hers roughly.

She squirmed, her arousal driving her insane. He started rocking into her, his hips slapping against hers. Then he reached down and stroked her clit.

"Now." His voice was low and gruff.

"Duke!" She let go as heat exploded over her skin and her body trembled, her insides rippling.

It seemed to trigger his release as he jerked his hips uncontrollably, calling out her name as he groaned. His body stilled, and his weight pressed onto her, as they caught their breaths. He pulled out, grabbed tissues from his desk and cleaned up.

He tossed the wipes into a bin and tucked his still-hard shaft back into his trousers.

Grabbing more tissues, he cleaned her and tidied her dress. Carla yelped when he lifted her, carried her over to the sofa and placed her on his lap. He brushed back the sweat-slicked hair from her face, his expression a little sad. "You know you've ruined me. What am I going to do about you?"

Warmth spread through her body. She smiled, tracing a finger down his arm. "You mean that you don't want anyone knowing that you're not a mean, sadistic man. That you actually care about me."

She said it as a joke. But the way he looked at her made her gasp. "You do actually care about me."

"Don't you get it? Indulging this thing between us could get you killed. I shouldn't have swapped your brother for you. He should be languishing in the dungeon."

Wow. He'd chosen her. He'd given up her brother, a more valuable hostage just so he could have her near. He'd sacrificed his advantage, his leverage, for her. Even when he'd been angry with her, he'd wanted her.

Nobody had ever chosen her over Marlon before. Not Daddy. No one.

"I understand," she said, cupping his chin, the stubble grating. "But I'd rather be with you and risk death than go back home and leave you to face death alone."

"That's good because now that you're here, I'm going to fight to keep you," he said, a sexy smile lit up his face as he leaned in for a slow kiss that sent her pulse racing again.

# TWENTY

CARLA'S STOMACH churned, and she shifted in the back seat of an SUV travelling along the Iguocha airport highway. Duke sat beside her while Mason and another man she didn't recognise were in front. They had just disembarked from the private aeroplane after a forty-five minutes flight from Opal City, on their way to visit Duke's uncle, Don Sylvester.

She had been excited about leaving the house for the first time since her arrival there. Now, the anticipation fizzled into agitation, anxiety threatening to get the better of her.

On the upside, her relationship with Duke had progressed over the past week. Given free rein of his home, she'd been introduced to household staff and local crewmembers. They lived like a couple, slept on the same bed, ate meals together and made love at any opportunity.

Anything she'd wanted had been delivered to her. Yesterday, a hairdresser had washed, treated and styled her hair in preparation for her trip. A beautician had given her a facial treatment, a manicure and a pedicure.

She hadn't left the house. However, there was enough space within the walled grounds of his house to prevent claustrophobia.

Her father hadn't called off the hit. She was still a hostage, in name only. Hence the reason for this visit to Duke's uncle.

Don Sylvester had sent an invitation to her father for a face-to-face meeting to discuss a deal with guaranteed safe passage. Daddy had accepted and had chosen a date—today. He had also requested proof of life and care, which was Carla in person.

So here she was, polished and perfect, in a gorgeous multi-coloured maxi silk dress, designer high-heeled sandals and sparkly diamond jewellery. She didn't look or feel like a prisoner. Hopefully, Daddy would see how happy she was and agree to the truce.

This part of the arrangement unsettled her.

A truce would mean going home. Yes, she would see her family and her friends. She'd missed her close friends, Ayo and Jemima. She hadn't been able to message them because Duke had said it was best to wait for the outcome of today's meeting.

Whatever the result, she didn't want to leave Duke. Could not imagine a future without him.

Thirty minutes later, the car slowed down when it reached a treelined street. They drove through open black metal gates with gilded arches. The long drive led up to a palatial house.

But she was a long way from the megacity she'd grown up in, and this location seemed rural.

The car came to a halt. Mason and the driver got out.

Carla reached for Duke's hand, her anxiety spiking. "Are you sure this is going to work?"

"Give us a minute," Duke said to the man who held the door open. The door closed before he turned to her and covered her hand with his. "I don't know what your father will say. But my uncle will give us an audience. That I can promise." He lifted her hand and pressed his soft lips to the back. "And if it doesn't work, then we'll move to Plan B."

Carla didn't ask what Plan B was for fear of jinxing Plan A. She suspected it involved Duke going to war with her father and shuddered at the thought.

Closing her eyes, she muttered a silent prayer. "Plan A, please work."

She opened her eyes as Duke pressed a kiss to her lips. "Come on."

Someone opened the door on her side. Carla swung her legs out and waited. Duke came around and helped her from the vehicle.

Holding her hand, they strode onto the portico and through the impressive looking front entrance.

"De Duke. I batala?" A woman about her age in a 50s style yellow and white polka-dot dress practically tumbled into Duke and embraced him.

"Sahara, it's good to see you." Duke returned the hug warmly, a grin on his face. He didn't let go of Carla's hand and steered the woman to face Carla. "I want you to meet someone. This is Carla."

"Oh. I've heard so much about you. It's nice to finally meet you," Sahara said, smiling at Carla.

"Same here," Carla replied. She'd worried about making a good impression with Duke's relatives when he spoke fondly of his uncle's daughter.

"Sahara is more of a baby sister than a cousin," Duke said, keeping arms around the two women.

"Uh," Sahara groaned and poked his side. "Enough of the 'baby sister' already."

Duke chuckled and teased. "You'll always be my baby sister."

Sahara's smile stayed on, and it was apparent the two of them had a good relationship.

"Don't mind him." Sahara turned her attention to Carla as they walked into the house.

"If it's any consolation," Carla said, glad to be included in their banter. "I have an older brother, and he is also a pain in the ass."

A pang squeezed her chest. She wished her relationship with Marlon was half as good as Sahara's relationship with Duke.

"Oh, I like her." Sahara laughed. "We're going to get along brilliantly. Omigod, is that what I think it is?"

She grabbed Carla's arm. The diamond and gold engagement ring caught the light and sparkled.

"Yes, it is," Carla said, squealing with excitement.

"Not too loud," Duke said in a low tone. "We haven't announced it because we wanted to tell Uncle first."

"Gurl, the two of us need to talk. I want the low down on how you snagged this man. When the men retire to discuss business as they always do, we are going to have a good old-fashioned girly chat."

Carla giggled. She really liked Duke's cousin. "Okay."

"Good." She led them into a spacious sitting room with cream upholstered settees and natural tone furnishings.

An older man in an embroidered navy tunic suit sat on one of the chairs. He had a patch of grey at the top edge of his otherwise black hair and a low, trimmed beard.

"Dad, De Duke is here," Sahara announced.

"Uncle," Duke finally let go of Carla and walked over.

"Duke." The man opened his arms and embraced his nephew before leaning back. "It's good to see you, son."

"Same here. You seem to be getting younger every time I see you," Duke said, looking the man over.

"I'm thankful for a good life." The old man looked past his nephew. "I see you brought a guest."

"Yes, Uncle." Duke stepped back and took Sahara's hand, leading her to where the man sat. "This is Carla Owo. I want to formally introduce her to you as the woman I'm going to marry."

Carla went down on her knees in full curtesy. "Good afternoon, Daddy."

She greeted him in the formal way she would treat an elder in her part of the country.

"Welcome, my daughter." If the man was surprised at Duke's announcement, he didn't show it. "Sit down."

Duke helped her up, and they both sat on the adjacent sofa to his uncle.

Servants showed up with refreshments. Easy conversation flowed, mainly focused around current affairs, small talk and laughter.

No one mentioned Carla's status. Anyone looking in would see a woman visiting her future in-laws with her fiancé.

"So, Carla, my daughter. I need the truth from you," Don Sylvester said.

Her stomach flipped over, and she glanced at Duke, who nodded at her. "Of course, Daddy. What about?"

"Regardless of who sired him, Duke is my son. We share blood."

"Yes. I understand."

"So, you will also understand that I am concerned about his proposal to marry you and what it will cost him."

Carla twisted her hands on her lap, unable to say anything. What could she say that would allay the old man's fears? She had caused Duke problems from the night they'd met. Could she really swear that she wouldn't be a burden to him in the future?

"I don't know if you've noticed it. But around here, the family is everything. And family means trust, honour, loyalty and love. They keep us together and more importantly; those things keep us alive."

He took a sip from the glass of water on the small side table.

"If Duke had made this proposal ten years ago, I would have forbidden it. So maybe it's old age or plain nostalgia talking now. After Duke called me last week, I spent time looking through old family photographs of my brother Daniel and I when we were young. He was idealistic and optimistic while I was pragmatic. We had disagreements. But he was my brother, and I loved him. When he introduced the woman, who would eventually become his wife and Duke's mother to me, we had another disagreement. I didn't want him to marry her. Because she was Yoruba."

Carla sucked in a sharp breath and glanced at Duke. She hadn't known this about Duke's mother.

Duke reached out and squeezed Carla's hand. "Uncle—"

"Let me finish, son. This was just after the war, after our people had been massacred in a genocide. The pain was still raw and harsh. So, when Daniel brought Bisola home, I was angry at him for choosing someone from a tribe we felt betrayed us. I thought their union would bring problems. But Daniel being Daniel, he saw the positive side of things. He thought their union would be a beacon of unity. In the end, only one thing swayed me—Bisola's love for Daniel and her dedication to our cause. My brother would not have become the great politician he became without Bisola."

He paused, staring at Carla with piercing eyes the same colour as Duke's.

"Now, I'm going to ask you the same question I asked Bisola. Are you willing to become part of this family and uphold our values, to share our challenges and dance at our celebrations?"

Carla opened her mouth to speak but shut it when Don Sylvester raised his hand.

"Think about it carefully. This life isn't for everyone. But once you're here, you need to commit to it."

Duke pulled out his buzzing phone from his jacket pocket, pressed a button and raised it to his ear. He listened for s few seconds and put the phone away. "The visitors are here."

Carla's heart slammed in her chest. Was her father here? Marlon?

"Good," Don Sylvester said. "Go and make them comfortable. I'll join you shortly."

"Yes, sir." Duke pushed off the sofa and held his hand out. "Come on, Carla."

She reached for him, and he pulled her up. They left the sitting room and walked across the lobby into another reception room.

"Jem!" Carla shrieked as soon as she saw her friend sitting beside Marlon on a sofa.

"Carla!" Her friend jumped off the sofa.

They met each other in the middle of the room and hugged tight.

Heat radiated from Carla's chest, and she felt breathless. Her friend was the last person she expected to see today. She leaned back. "I can't believe you're here. It's so good to see you."

"I had to come and see you." Jemima pulled back and looked her over. "You look great."

Even weirder, Marlon was smiling at her. He pulled her into a hug. "It's good to see you, sis."

Carla hid her shock as her brother's cologne filled her nostrils.

"Nice to see you," she said as she pulled back. "Is Daddy here?"

"No," her brother said. "I came on his behalf."

"Oh," She replied, kinda relieved she didn't have to face her father. "Is he well?"

"Yes. He's doing great."

"I'll leave you to talk to your brother," Duke said.

"That's not necessary," Marlon said. "The ladies can chat amongst themselves while we discuss business."

"Is it okay if Carla and I go down to the beach?" Jemima asked, holding onto Carla's hand.

"That's not a good idea," Duke said.

"Oh." Jemima's face fell, her bottom lip stuck out.

Carla turned to Duke. "Please. Let us go to the beach."

"I'll be with them, and we can go with some of the bodyguards," Sahara added.

Duke sighed. "Okay. I'll arrange for some of the men to go with you."

"Thank you." Carla leaned in and kissed him of the cheek before he left the room with Marlon.

Ten minutes later, Carla, Jemima and Sahara sat in the back of a seven-seater SUV. Jide sat in the front passenger seat, and another man who was introduced as Nnamdi drove the vehicle. They arrived at the harbour and boarded a yacht that belonged to Sahara's father to take them to the remote Ifoko location.

They arrived at the beach. People sat on blankets on the grass, eating, reading, and chatting. Kids played ball games. They strolled to the café built like an octagonal-shaped cabin with a thatched roof, standing on stilts.

"Grab a table. I'll order refreshments. What would you like?" Sahara asked.

"Iced tea and lemon cake," Carla said.

"Iced coffee and caramel waffle," Jem said.

They found a table under a shaded tree and settled on it. The bodyguards stood around them. Sea waves crashing on the sandy shore a few metres away.

"This place is beautiful," Jem said.

"I know," Carla said.

Sahara brought the refreshments. They chatted for a while and watched people cavorting around the beach.

"How did you know where I was?" Carla asked.

"Ayo and I got worried when you didn't respond to any of our messages. I called your phone and went to your house when I couldn't reach you. Marlon told me you'd gone on a trip. Then a few days ago, he came to see me and asked me to come to Iguocha with him to see you."

"Marlon invited you to come with him? I didn't know you two were that tight."

"We've been spending more time together since you went away."

Carla's state of shock returned. Marlon who never gave her any time of day was suddenly interested in her friends. It was too good to believe.

Carla reached for her friend's hand. "Be careful with my brother. I don't want you to get hurt by him."

"Ah. You worry too much. Marlon has been nice to me. A perfect gentleman." Jem said.

"If you say so." She stood up. "Excuse me. I'm going to get some ice cream. Want one."

"None for me," Sahara said.

"Chocolate ice cream for me.

"See you in a minute." She headed towards the café. Jide followed her. "You don't have to come with me. We're on a remote beach with only one café. I'll be fine."

"Okay. I'll wait out here," he said.

"Do you want some ice cream?" she asked.

"No, thanks."

She went inside and joined the short queue for the counter.

Something prodded her back. Someone didn't understand personal boundaries.

Shifting, she glanced back, ready to tell the person off. Her muscles froze.

"Don't make a sound. I've got a gun, and I will use it." Abdul grabbed her with his left hand, the right hand hidden inside a satchel slung across his shoulder. He dragged her through a different entrance marked 'Staff Only'.

"What are you doing? Let me go." She struggled.

He ignored her protests and those of the kitchen staff as he hauled her to the back exit.

"If you don't tell me what's going on, I'm going to scream." She dug her heels into the sands, refusing to budge.

"I've been sent to take you home." He tugged again.

Surprised, she stumbled forward. "Daddy sent you?"

She glanced around, expecting to see more men. If her father sent Abdul, then his goons should be here. Those men travelled in packs like wolves.

Nodding, he hooked hand over her shoulder and steered away from the security men towards the trees.

"But I can't go back home. Marlon is with Duke's uncle, negotiating a deal."

She dug her heels in again. She couldn't go home while her father was still hunting Duke. She couldn't abandon him. Anyway, he was with Marlon right now negotiating a deal to resolve the feud.

Abdul laughed derisively. "You're so naïve if you think that's what he's doing."

She stiffened. Dread sat like rocks in her belly. "What does that mean?"

"What do you care?"

"Duke is my fiancé. We are engaged." She raised her hand so he could see the engagement ring. "See?"

He smacked her across the face. "I'm going to kill him. I swear it."

Pain and shock made her body lax. She grabbed her burning face.

Two giggling girls ran out of the woods and froze with fear.

Abdul swivelled, gun pointing at them.

Without thinking, Carla stepped into the line of fire and shouted. "Run!"

The kids ran back in the direction they'd come.

"What the fuck are you doing? They were just children." She yelled at Abdul, who kept dragging her. She should have taken up those self-defence classes Duke had suggested months ago.

"I don't care. I—"

"Let her go!"

She swivelled as Jide ran towards them. A cracking sound exploded through the air, and Carla screamed.

# TWENTY-ONE

ROLLING HIS neck to work off the stiffness, Duke tried not to give in to his rising annoyance. He sat in a comfortable leather chair with Mason covering his flank.

Not that he expected hostility. Not that he wouldn't be able to handle it if it came up.

This was Sylvester Odili's house, his uncle and adoptive father. This was home away from home. The place he'd spent his formative years.

Although he now ran his own successful businesses, Duke would never disrespect the man who had raised him like a son. He regularly sought the elder's advice on weighted issues.

Hence he'd consulted his uncle with the idea of brokering a peace deal with John Bull Owo by uniting the Odili and Owo families in marriage.

Don Sylvester had been sceptical, and he had valid reasons, considering their family history. His uncle believed the death of Duke's parents was linked to their inter-tribal union. Duke couldn't argue otherwise, although the private investigator he hired said the method of assassination seemed personal. Instead of ambushed gunfire or a car bomb, his father had been shot close range while his mother's throat had been cut, in their home. It seemed the person wanted them to see their killer up close.

Duke's pulse sped up, and he clenched his hands. When he found the person responsible, he would make sure they saw his face before he delivered retribution.

Bernard Ojiaku, Don Sylvester's adviser, walked into the room and strode over to where Marlon sat. He murmured something Duke couldn't hear before Marlon stood and followed him out.

In the scheme of things, sitting out here while Marlon went in to see Don Sylvester would've unsettled a lesser man. But Duke was confident about his place here. He had already discussed matters with the old man. The Baron via Marlon was entitled to air his grievances in private before Duke was called into the meeting.

His phone buzzed. He fished it out of his pocket and glanced at the screen. Jide.

Cold fingers slithered down Duke's spine. Jide would not call him while he was in a meeting with Don Sylvester unless it was an emergency.

He answered the call immediately. "Jide, what's wrong?"

"Something happened," he said.

Duke shot off the chair. Dread made his stomach roll. "What do you mean, something happened?"

"Someone tried to abduct Carla."

"Fuck." Duke headed for the balcony doors.

"She's okay. But I got shot. We're on the boat back to the harbour."

"I'm on my way." He ended the call.

Mason followed him. "What's going on?"

"Someone tried to abduct Carla, and Jide was hit." Duke hurried towards the vehicles parked under the carport.

"We need to get to the harbour," he said to the man who'd driven them from the airport."

"Yes, Sir." The man ran to the car.

Duke turned to another security man. "Tell Don Bernard I had to go deal with an emergency. I'll be back as soon as I can."

The man nodded as Duke got into the vehicle. Mason joined him in the back seat, and the car sped out of the drive, in a flurry of gravel.

Duke couldn't shake the sense of dread although Jide had said Carla was okay.

His engagement to Carla was a pre-emptive strike. Getting the approval from his uncle was the ace up his sleeve. No one could argue with what amounted to an edict from one of the highest-ranking members of the Yadili.

Yet she could be taken away from him.

He could not lose her. He who couldn't get attached to people had made a connection he couldn't detach. He who had been labelled emotionally unavailable was fully present in a relationship.

Carla was his obsession, his drug. He was addicted to her.

He couldn't contemplate giving her up. The woman whom no one else wanted for him.

"What actually happened?" Mason asked, drawing him from his musings.

"I don't know." Duke scrubbed hands over his face, swallowing with difficulty.

"But who would want to take Carla?"

"The only people who knew she would be here are the Owos and us."

"Do you think this is John Bull's doing? His men are in Iguocha with Don Sylvester's invitation. They could have followed the ladies when they went to the beach."

"Go faster!" Duke yelled at the driver, his usual calm exterior exploding. Being away from Carla was killing him.

The car whizzed through the streets, and they pulled into the harbour parking within twenty minutes.

Duke got out of the car and ran towards the boats. He got onto jetty as the yacht pulled in and climbed onboard.

Jide sat in a lounging chair on the main deck, his shirt sleeve torn, and a clean bandage wrapped around his upper arm. He tried to move. "Boss."

"Don't get up. How are you doing?" Duke asked as he looked around.

"I'm okay. The boat medic dressed the wound. Said I would need sutures at the hospital. But I'll live."

"Good," Duke replied.

Footsteps clattered down the stairs from the top deck. Nnamdi, one of the Odili crews that worked for the old man appeared first. Then the women followed.

Carla ran over and crashed into him. Relief washed over him.

"You don't know how happy I am to see you," she said in a shaky voice.

"I'm here now." He hugged her tight, not caring about the public display and what the men would think about him. First was making sure she was unharmed, the second item was making sure they all knew she belonged to him now. Lastly, was understanding what went wrong today and fixing it, so it never happened again.

Across the deck, Mason questioned Jide about what happened.

"We were sitting at one of the outside tables when Carla went to the café to buy some ice cream," Jide said. "I went into the shop five minutes later. She wasn't there. I rushed out and instructed Nnamdi to search the beach while I went inland. I found Carla struggling with a man I didn't recognise. When I intervened, the man shot me. Luckily Nnamdi arrived at the same time and tried to tackle the man, but he managed to escape."

"Who the fuck was he?" Mason barked angrily, glanced from the women to the men.

Sahara shrugged and lifted her hands. "Don't look at me. I've never seen him before."

Jemima bowed her head, averting her gaze.

Duke's spine prickled, and he narrowed his eyes. Did the woman know something? "Jemima, do you know the man?"

Carla tugged Duke's arm and muttered, "I know who he is."

Duke glanced down, frowning. "Who?"

"It was Abdul."

Duke stiffened, pulling away. "Abdul Sani?"

She nodded. "He said Daddy sent him to get me."

That only meant one thing. The Owos didn't want a peaceful resolution. They had sent Marlon as a distraction for Abdul to abduct Carla.

Duke lost his temper, pacing. "That muthafucka was here? In Iguocha? Trying to take you? That's why she's here." He pointed at Carla's friend. "She was the bait, sent to get you out of the house."

"No!" Carla refuted, shaking her head. "She wouldn't. Jem, tell him."

Her friend looked shamefaced. "I'm sorry, Carla. Marlon said they were keeping you here without your consent. He said this was the best way to get you out and that I should invite you to the beach or the shops. Abdul would do the rest. I sent him a message when we left the house."

"Fuck," Duke cursed out loud. He was done with negotiating for peace. If John Bull wanted a war, he would get one.

"Jem, I'm here because I want to be. I don't want to go back to Lori Osa."

"Really? You want to stay?"

"Yes." Carla took Duke's hand. "I love Duke. We're getting married."

"Come on," Duke said, not wanting to listen to her friend. "We need to get out of here."

He didn't know what else the Owos had in store, but this yacht on a secluded harbour wasn't the safest. The stakes were raised with a near abduction and one of his men getting shot. He needed to get Carla back to safety.

"Is Marlon still with Don Sylvester?" he asked.

"No. He left already," Mason replied. "Do you want me to send the men to look for him?"

"No." A much as he wanted to string Marlon and his father up, he couldn't start a war in Odili territory. That would be disrespectful to the old man. "We'll deal with the Owos later. I'm going to take Carla back to Opal City."

"Okay. I'll call the flight crew."

"Get it done. I want to be gone as soon as possible."

# TWENTY-TWO

THE FLIGHT back to Opal City was tense. Carla and Duke sat opposite each other on the plane. For the first time since she met the man, she saw how rattled he was.

Duke hadn't said much. Unlike the trips he spent in discussion with Mason, this time he stayed close to Carla throughout. It was as if he was afraid she would disappear if he turned away.

By the time they arrived at his house, it was already dark.

Carla left Duke downstairs while she went up to the bedroom. She stripped off and went into the shower. When she got out, she wrapped a towel around her body.

Duke walked into the bedroom. He still looked distracted and worried as he scrubbed his palm over his head and paced the room.

He was always the one taking care of her.

Carla wanted to do something for him. To show that they were on this path together, no matter where it led.

"Bae, you must be exhausted." She approached him and cupped his face. Why don't you take a shower and let me give you a massage?"

"You want to give me a massage?" He smiled down at her. "Have you done it before?"

"No. But how hard can it be? Go on." She pushed him towards the bathroom.

Still smiling, he kissed the corner of her mouth. "Okay."

He strode to the bathroom and shut the door.

She paced the bedroom, suddenly a ball of nervous energy. Her hands shook, and she panted. Today had been crazy. To think that they had started the day on a positive note, thinking that finally there would be a resolution between Duke and Daddy. Only for her to be ambushed by Abdul.

She seemed to have made a good impression with Duke's uncle, and she had seen her friend Jemima. Although her friend had been unwittingly involved in the kidnapping plot.

Her heart pounded. She took a few calming breaths to release the knot in her gut. She wanted to be comfortable without being naked. The point was to get Duke to relax and forget his worries tonight. She pulled on a crop top and panties.

Duke came out, covered in only a blue towel around his waist. He was tall, broad-chested.

Muscled ripped like an athlete, a little trail of hair dipped in a V shape and disappeared into the towel. Having witnessed one of his men getting shot today, she could imagine where the scars on his body came from.

Her breath caught in her throat. Damn. He always took her breath away.

His eyes rake over her body, and he bit his bottom lip. "Where do you want me?"

"In the middle of the bed." She pointed at it, before picking up the coconut oil jar she used for her body and hair.

Smirking, he dropped his towel, strode to the bed and parked himself in the middle face down.

She climbed the bed and knelt beside him.

He glanced at her. "Sit on me."

Her heart skipped a beat at the sexual connotation, although he said it innocently.

She moved into position astride his hips.

"That's good." Exhaling a sigh, he closed his eyes.

"Good? I haven't done anything yet." She opened the jar, tipped some oil into her palm and placed the item within easy reach on the mattress. Then she rubbed her palm together as she'd seen her masseuse do.

"Something happens to me when you touch me," he said. "Especially when you lean your body against mine. It's grounding and calming."

"That's good to know." His words emboldened her. She slid her palms up his back. "You have a similar effect on me too."

He let out another sigh as she continued rubbing his back muscles, then his shoulders and upper arms. She doubted she was as good as the professionals. But his body had lost some of the tension he'd carried all day.

"Turn over," she said.

Like a meek lamb, he moved. He rolled, shifting her, so he was on his back, and she straddled his dark, broad semi-hard erection, legs around his hips.

She'd never thought she could be with a man who would leave himself like putty in her hands.

Duke was perfect. In body. In spirit. He was a walking, talking turn-on.

Her libido rose to a fever pitch. Her hands roam the toned muscles of his abs, pecs and over his shoulders. She lowered her head and kissed him.

He didn't take over, allowing her tongue and mouth to explore his. For a while, his touch feathered her skin as they enjoyed the feel of each other's bodies.

With a groan, he angled his mouth, deepened the kiss and tugged her hips, so her pussy ground over his engorged dick.

She moaned, her body coming alive under his magical caresses. She wanted so much from him, to feel him, inside as well as out.

She reached for more oil and then down between their bodies and wrapped her hand around his swollen length. He pulsated, thick and hard, her fingers not an exact fit for his girth.

Her insides clenched. She whimpered, kissing him desperately while stroking him slowly.

"Cara," he groaned, his tone a prayer and a plea.

His words were like a shot of aphrodisiac and endorphins. She tugged him.

Another guttural sound escaped him, and he closed his eyes. "I thought you're supposed to be giving me a massage."

She giggled and kept stroking up and down. "This part of your anatomy also needs attention."

He chuckled, eyes flickering with lust. "I won't argue with that."

Then he moved his hips in rhythm, pumping into her oiled hand. The evidence of his arousal leaked and mixed with the coconut oil in her grip. Through it all, he didn't try to take over, his hands on her thighs were loose.

Her insides turned to liquid, her thongs barely a barrier for her juices. She'd never met a man like this. A man who wasn't afraid to be vulnerable in her presence. Who wasn't scared to be open and expressive.

She loved that she could do this to him, for him. That she could take care of him. She could be wild and spontaneous when she wanted but taking care of someone else like this wasn't something she thought about usually.

"I love doing this to you," she whispered and locked lips with him. She covered his balls with her free hand, cupped and squeezed.

"Unh," he groaned, closing his eyes, his breathing ragged. "You're going to make me come."

"That's exactly what I want," she whispered close to his ear and tightened her grip on his dick and stroked him hard over and over.

Shuddering, he gripped her nape, dragged her face to his. "This one is for you."

He gave her a kiss that would leave her lips swollen as his hips jerked uncontrollably and warm cum splattered onto her hand.

She kept pumping until he emptied out and his breathing turned to pants, his eyes rolling back in his head.

He held her forehead to his as he caught his breath. Then he brushed his lips against hers, tenderly.

Euphoria buzzed through her, although she wasn't the one who climaxed.

"Come here," he said, his voice still husky as he lifted her. "Sit on my face."

She shifted until her pussy hovered over his mouth.

He tugged her thong aside. "Hold yourself open for me, will you."

She didn't need a second invitation. Using her fingers, she tugged her labia apart, exposing her swollen clit to his gaze.

"You're so fucking pretty." He slid fingers inside her and curled them, massaging her sweet spot. He used his mouth to great effect, licking and sucking her clit over and over.

Her whole body squirmed and writhed. She rode his face while he fucked her with fingers and tongue. Soon she was soaring on a wave of orgasm over orgasm until sensitivity made her fall onto the bed.

He reached down, grabbed the discarded towel and cleaned them both up before chucking it away.

Afterwards, they curled up, facing each other, just content to be with each other, while they kissed gently for a while.

"Do you know why I sent you away the night we met at Arufin?" he murmured; eyes still closed. "Your eyes. The hazel colour reminded me of my mother's eyes. There are days when I miss her so much, it hurts. The day I met you, I'd been thinking about her. And then I saw you that night. I don't know. It's ridiculous because you probably hadn't been born when she died."

Although he tried to mask it, there were tendrils of pain in his statement. And he had been just a boy when he lost his parents, so surely he'd hurt.

"I'm sorry." She leaned down and pressed gentle kisses on his shoulder. "It's not ridiculous. Our ancestors believed that souls reincarnate. Maybe the soul that inhabited your mother's body now lives in mine. After all, the eyes are the windows of the soul. So maybe, that's what you saw when you first saw me."

He didn't say anything for what seemed like minutes but was probably just heart-thumping seconds. Had she overstepped?

"How do you know about reincarnation?" he asked.

She puffed out a relieved breath. "My friend, Ayo, is the daughter of an Ifá priestess and educates me regularly on African spirituality."

"Over here, we have Odinani, and I'm a practitioner. I've wondered why I feel so strongly about you. But what you said about reincarnation makes perfect sense to me. It's the reason I can't let you go. Do you understand?"

He gripped her hips. His gaze burned into her. The air around them swirled, sizzled with electricity.

"I understand. I don't want you to ever let me go" she whispered, heart racing.

She wanted him, wanted every inch of him, his body, his heart, his life.

He lifted his hand, stroked her chin and cheek with the back on his knuckle. "You told me you were in love with me. I'm not complaining. But why do you love me?"

"At first, it was just a physical attraction. You're a gorgeous man, and I wanted you. But then you saved me when you thought I was in trouble. In the car, you didn't paw me or try to get into my panties like other men do. You were different from the kind of people in my life."

"But I took you from your family—"

"Because my father tried to kill you."

"And I had you locked up and punished."

"Because I broke the rules and disrespected you. My actions put you in danger. If you hadn't punished me, my life and yours would be forfeit. I know how these things work."

He tilted his head on the pillow, studying her in silence. "We haven't talked about this. But now is a good time as any. Why did you offer Emmanuel sex? Where you really that desperate for blow?"

Shame washed over her, heating her skin. She turned her head away and shifted. His grip on her chin and hips tightened. She couldn't escape.

"I'm not going to force you to explain, but I need to understand why."

She sighed in resignation. "You need an explanation. First, I never intended to sleep with Emmanuel. I thought I'd be able to convince him to take one of the dresses as payment. Now, thinking back, it makes no sense, I know. But I was desperate for the blow. I didn't want to be in my head."

Her shoulders curled in, and her head bowed.

"Because you were locked in the room? You were safer in that room than wandering around the house in my absence. My men saw you as the enemy. I had to go on a business trip, and that was the only way I could think to keep you safe until I returned."

"I know now. But at the time I didn't know it was for my own good. Honestly, I didn't even care that it was for my own good. I just saw those four white walls, and they reminded me of when I was locked up at the Lori Osa sanatorium."

Duke stiffened. "Wait... What?"

She climbed off him, and this time he let her move. She flopped on the bed on her side, pulling her legs up and wrapping her arms around it.

He scooped her onto his body, wrapping his arms around her. "Why were you in the sanatorium?"

Tears pooled and dripped onto his chest. "After my mother died, I had very vivid dreams about her death. I told everyone that Daddy killed her. But my father said that I was sick and hallucinating. He sent me to a doctor who said I was suffering from psychosis due to the trauma of my mother's death. He recommended that I be sent to the sanatorium for treatment. I was there for almost a year."

"Fuck!" he swore in a low voice, and his grip on her tightened.

"Good thing, though. The dreams about my father killing my mother stopped, and for a long time, I didn't have them. Sometimes they come back. But I've learned never to discuss them with anyone, afraid my father will send me back there. He's threatened to do that several times."

"What the fuck? Your father threatens to send you to a mental institution?"

"He does that whenever he wants me to comply with his orders. That's why I agreed to marry Abdul. He had a warrant from a judge sectioning me and threatened to use it."

"Your father is sick. I'm never going to let him hurt you again," he vowed.

"I know." Carla curled up beside him, hand on his chest.

His heart thumped in a steady rhythm against her palm, his skin warm, his scent in her nostril.

"How do you feel about getting married tomorrow?" he said in a quiet voice.

"Tomorrow?" She sat upright.

He leaned on his elbow, his dark eyes searching her face. "You still want to get married, don't you?"

"Yes, Bae. I'd marry you tomorrow if it was possible. But nothing has been arranged." Frowning, she crossed her arms over her chest. She wanted a wedding with all the trimmings.

"What do you need to arrange for a wedding?" He matched her posture, sitting up and facing her.

"I don't have a dress, a venue, catering, invitations, my friends." She counted the items off on her fingers.

"All those things are important to you?"

"Well, yes. Aren't they important to you?"

"No. The important things to me at our wedding are—" He lifted her hand and counted off the fingers "—you, me and the officiator. Everything else is extra." He pressed soft lips to her knuckles, sending tingles down her spine.

Her resistance melted a little. "Even if we leave out the extras, where are we going to get a priest at such short notice."

He leaned sideways and grabbed his phone from the cabinet. "I can call one and find out."

She tilted her head, bemused. "You have a priest? I didn't know you go to church."

"She is a priestess of Ani, the Earth Goddess."

"And you can call her on your phone?"

"Can you call your parish priest on the phone?"

"I guess so although I've never tried to call him."

"She's a human being, you know. She eats, sleeps and has a life like any other person. The only difference is that she is the local custodian of any ritual ceremonies to Ani."

"And you think she'll be free tomorrow?"

"I can call her and find out."

A little agitated, she got off the bed and walked to the window. She had turned the low, deep sill into a loveseat by adding pillows. During the day, the view of the valley was stunning. Right now, yellow lights dotted and blinked in the distance.

She sat on the sill, pulled her leg up, wrapped her arms around her legs and tucked her chin on her knees.

Duke shifted to the end of the bed, feet on the rug, arms braced on his thighs. "You don't want me to call her."

She sighed, unsure about how to explain her feelings. "It's just ... I've dreamt about a big wedding for a long time. At first, it was pure fantasy about this prince who would whisk me away from my life, and we would have a fairy tale wedding. Then every time I saw a wedding photo on social media, I would think about how my own wedding would be more extravagant. How everything would be on point."

She puffed out another deep breath. "Your idea of an intimate ceremony with just you and me taking our vows is beautiful and romantic."

He rubbed his palms over his face. "You think so?"

"Yes. It is. It's just not my dream wedding. I know it's selfish, but I want a big fat Nigerian wedding. You can chalk it down to me being Yoruba and how we love to party."

Chuckling, he pushed off the bed and strode across the room in her direction, still naked. The rippling of toned muscles, his fluid gait and the well-hung semi scrambled her brain.

Her temperature rose, pulse rate spiked, and she forgot how to breathe.

He scooped her up and sat on the loveseat. His legs were longer than hers. They couldn't sit facing each other along the bench. Instead, he lowered her astride his lap, while his feet stayed on the floor. She wrapped her hands around his neck, and his dick prodded her bum.

"So Yoruba people love to party. Lift your arms for me." He lifted the hem of her t-shirt and tugged it over her head with her compliance.

She'd forgotten what they'd been discussing. "That's actually a stereotype. I only said it as a joke to make you smile." There were many of her people who didn't like to party.

"I know." Grinning, he cupped her left boob, lowered his head and flicked his tongue on her nipple.

"Oh," she moaned, and he repeated the action, his left hand holding the arch of her back.

"How about two weddings?" He trailed caresses with his lips up to her collarbone. "An intimate one now and an extravagant one later when we've settled the feud with your father."

The things he was doing to her made her slow in absorbing his words. "We can have two weddings?"

"Of course. I don't want to deny you the fairy-tale event you want. But I don't want to wait any longer to make you my wife. I want to give you the protection that comes with being a part of my family, and I can add you to my will. So, if something happens to me, you will still be protected."

She stiffened and grabbed his head with both hands, making him look up. "Nothing is going to happen to you."

"I hope so. But let's face it. Your father is still trying to kill me, and he might succeed."

"No! I reject it." She pulled him close and wrapped her arms tight around his neck, tears clouding her eyes.

"So do I." He held her, hand stroking gently down her back.

"So, you really want to add me to your will?" she murmured against his shoulder.

"Yes. I promised to always take care of you. And I need to keep doing it if I'm not here."

Her throat clogged up with more tears, and she leaned back, caressing his cheek and neck. How did she get lucky? "Then let's get married tomorrow."

"You mean it? We don't have to if you're not ready?"

"Oh. I'm ready." She leaned in and kissed him with all her heart.

Passion blazed. Kisses turned to caresses. Soon she rode his dick, bouncing on the loveseat, the backdrop of lights twinkling in the valley.

# TWENTY-THREE

TWO DAYS later, the phone rang as Duke got out of the shower. No ID showed up. He entered the code to trace the call before he picked it anyway.

"Is this Duke Odili?" a man asked.

The noise in the background sounded like a public location.

"Yes. Who is this?"

"You don't know who I am, Mr Odili, but I have important information for you. Can you meet me?"

He sounded agitated. Was this a tactic to draw Duke out in the open. He could not forget what happened at Ujam's ranch. This could be another ambush.

"You should tell me whatever you want to say on the phone."

"Mr Odili, I know you have little reason to trust me. But this is important. Your life is in danger."

His words were rushed. Duke pictured his gaze darting around furtively.

"There's nothing new there. I have better things to do."

Without the direct threat from The Baron, his life was in danger from other sources, including corrupt public officials.

"I believe Mazi Daniel Odili was your father, and Oganiru Njoku worked for him," he said in a low tone.

Duke froze, and memories of his childhood came rushing back. Standing by the window, watching Oganiru as he patrolled their house at night. "Yes. What do you know about him?"

"Oganiru Njoku was my father."

Duke's body rocked from the shock of his statement. Oganiru or Niru as he'd been known had worked for his father. After his parents' death, Niru had smuggled him out of danger and taken him to his uncle. He hadn't seen the man again.

"Are you in Opal City?" Duke asked.

"Yes," he replied.

"Meet me at Mocha Cafe on Ugwo Street in one hour."

Duke hung up and called Maddox.

"Arrange surveillance around Mocha Café. I have a meeting there in one hour. I will need Jide in the house with Fabian and Lebechi watching over Carla."

"Yes, Boss," he replied. Maddox was the enforcer so arranging security at short notice was nothing to him.

Carla came out of the bathroom, her expression unhappy. "Are you going out without me? Take me with you."

"I can't." Duke couldn't risk it in case this was a setup.

"You promised this week was for me, and there would be no business." She pouted; her gaze lowered to the floor.

Sighing heavily, Duke walked up to her and tilted her chin up, so she met his gaze. "I know what I said. But something came up."

"Can't it wait?" she asked.

"No, it can't. I'll make it up to you when I get back."

"Promise?"

"Promise." He tangled fingers into her hair and tugged her close, kissing her. She tried to deepen the kiss, but he didn't let her. He had to leave shortly.

"Jide is going to stay with you. Don't leave the house without him. I'm not expecting trouble here. But in case there is any, do what he says. He'll keep you safe."

"Okay."

He brushed his lips against her forehead before getting dressed quickly.

As he left the house, Carla stood at the door watching them. A part of him wished he wasn't going out, especially so soon after an attempted abduction. But he needed to find out what Mr Njoku knew about his parents' death.

Mason was already in the backseat of the car waiting. Maddox drove.

"What's this about?" Mason asked as the SUV exited the drive onto the curvy road leading into town.

"I'm not sure yet. But it's something to do with my parents' death."

"It could be an ambush."

"I've thought about that, and I don't think it's an ambush. But just in case, I want you outside the café. I'll go in alone. Who do we have watching the place?"

"I sent Mike and Obiora out there when you called," Maddox said. "Mike reported, saying there was nothing unusual."

Good news. But Duke could not relax.

The coffee shop was in a corner lot of a residential street with old-style buildings of yellowed walls and red roofs. This was smack bang in the middle of Odili turf, so the people were loyal. They drove up the street to find children playing football in a small common area no larger than a block. Maddox parked the car in front of the building.

"Mike is on a roof across the road and Obiora is at the back," Mason said.

Nodding, Duke stepped out of the vehicle. Maddox left the car and disappeared round the corner. A football flew in the air and landed in front of Duke on the pavement. He caught it with both hands as two boys not much older than ten years old ran across the tarred street.

"Mazi, ndewo," the taller one said. "Ewena iwe. Biko nye m bọlụ."

This was part of the Igbo heartland, and most residents conversed in the local language.

"Jiri nwayọọ ka ị ghapu imebi ihe ọ bụna," Duke replied, acknowledging his apology and request for the return of his football, and telling him to take it easy so he didn't break anything. He patted the shorter kid on the head as he handed the ball over.

"Daalụ," the smaller one replied while the older stared from Mason back to Duke.

Duke squatted before them so he could be at eye level. "Do you live close by?"

They both nodded.

"Go and play indoors for the next hour." He looked up at where their friends stood watching what was going on. "And tell your friends to do the same. No one should come out for the next hour."

He straightened up. "Do you understand?"

"Ehe!" They both ran off.

Duke watched as they spoke to their friends, and then the group of kids all ran toward different houses. Confident that no child would be harmed if this turned out to be a battle, he turned to Mason.

"The team are in position, and it's all clear." His friend said.

Duke walked into the café while Mason waited outside.

It was quiet at this time of the day. A group of teenagers sat at one end.

In the other direction, a hooded man sat by the window. He stood up as Duke crossed the threshold and walked to the back to sit in a more private booth. He was dressed in jeans, a black, hooded long-sleeve top, and black boots.

Duke strode down the aisle and slid into the seat opposite the man. He didn't like sitting with his back to the door. But Mason and the men were watching his flank.

"Mr Njoku," Duke said.

"Ebuka. My name is Ebuka."

He wasn't burly but had tight, hard muscles beneath his clothes. His face had sharp planes. His eyes were those of a man who'd seen hard times.

The waitress dressed in a white t-shirt with the café logo and black skirt came around. She was probably in her late thirties. Her braided hair was packed into a top bun, and she had barely-there makeup on her face. A ring on her finger announced she was married and with the roundness of her curves, she had probably carried babies, too.

What if she got hurt because of him? He couldn't leave her children without a mother.

"Nnọọ. Kedu ihe ga-amasị gị?" she welcomed, asking what they would like.

Duke read her name tag, pulled out a wad of bills from his pocket and looked into her eyes. "Ifeoma, please bring us two bottles of malt. Send everyone else out, and this is for your troubles."

He tucked the notes into the pocket of her apron. There was enough in there to pay for any repair required for the place.

"It's not necessary, Mr Odili," she spoke in English this time. "You helped us when we have problems with the landlord."

A couple of years previously, the landlord had hiked up the rent and made it unaffordable for the locals. He'd threatened to lock them up if they didn't pay up. They'd petitioned Duke who bought properties on the street and fixed the rent at the rate it had been before the hike. Duke was still making enough money to cover the mortgage used to buy the strip. And he'd earned the loyalty of the community in the process.

"Keep it," Duke insisted. If nothing else, it would buy her silence when law enforcement started asking questions.

"Daalụ," she said before walking off to do his bidding.

The teenagers left in a hurry as she ushered them out and flipped the sign to 'Closed'.

Duke relaxed into the seat, projecting outward confidence. He listened for any sounds out of the ordinary. Outside, tyres crunched on the tarmac as a car went by. Footsteps quickened.

Probably someone who'd spotted Mason standing outside and decided to hurry along.

Inside, the ceiling fan whirred. The fridge door thudded close.

Mr Njoku assumed a non-threatening pose, his hands atop of the table. He didn't fidget. But his muscles were tense, and he sat straight-backed, his shoulders squared. He looked as if he were expecting an attack at any moment. Neither of them said anything until Ifeoma returned with the drinks.

Her hands shook as she laid the cold drinks on the table.

Duke placed his hand on her arm gently. "Take the rest of the day off."

She swallowed, nodded and walked behind the counter. She grabbed a bag off a shelf and hurried down the corridor. The back door squeaked indicating she'd walked out.

The man in front of him sipped his drink quietly from the glass.

"So, Ebuka, what is this about?" Duke asked before pouring the dark liquid into the transparent glass tumbler.

A thick layer of crema sat at the top of the dark brown liquid. He savoured the sweet taste before swallowing.

Ebuka lowered his cup and leaned back into his seat.

"There's a plot to assassinate you." He steepled his fingers with his elbows on the table.

Duke returned the glass onto the wooden coaster in a deliberate motion. He stretched his left hand across the seat top, right hand on the table, within easy reach of the handgun inside his jacket.

"As I said on the phone, there's nothing new there. What I don't understand is why you feel the need to warn me about it."

Other people would want to know who wanted them dead. However, Duke was interested in this man's motive for being here.

The man closed his eyes momentarily and raised his hands to his tired-looking face. He suddenly appeared older, although he couldn't be more than thirty years old. When he lowered his hands, something akin to regret flickered in his dark gaze.

"Because your father gave my family all they have. My father, Oganiru, worked for Daniel Odili. Papa spoke very fondly about your dad, rest their souls, especially in his last days." He made the sign of the cross, touching his forehead, chest, and both shoulders. "His one regret in life seemed to be that he couldn't save your family from the tragedy that happened."

"But your father smuggled me out of the house and hid me until he could get me safely to my uncle. He saved my life."

"Yes. He told me that when he started working for your father, his one responsibility was to keep you safe. He swore to do that even if it meant giving up his life. But he also wished he could have saved your parents as well."

Duke nodded as sadness washed over him. "Your father did what he was meant to do. He did his best from what I remember. The house was overrun. We were lucky to get out alive."

His eyes widened, his brows lifting.

Duke continued, "But my concern is that the people responsible were never found and justice was never served for my parents."

"I understand which is partly why I'm here. I don't want what happened to your parents to happen to you." He leaned back into his seat, stretching his arms wide to mirror the pose. "As soon as I heard your name, the memories of my father's stories came rushing back. What was the likelihood that a Duke Odili was on a hit list to be assassinated? Similar to the way Daniel Odili was killed."

Duke's head jerked back, and his muscles tensed at the implications of those words.

For a moment, he was a kid again witnessing his mother's murder.

Ebuka nodded. "Yes. Papa thought your parents were assassinated. It was too much of a coincidence to ignore, which is why I want to help you."

With furrowed brows and pursed lips, Duke lifted his chin. "How?"

"The how, I am yet to work out exactly."

"So, what's in it for you?" Duke was a businessman. No one ever gave anything for nothing.

"Your father was a great man. As a governor, our state flourished and most of the infrastructures he built form the backbone of the existing network in this region. He would have been a great president for this country if he hadn't been killed. He had great plans for the people, but he was killed because there were men who'd lose out if his plans came to fruition. I believe this country needs men like your father, and I think you could accomplish what your father planned to do."

Duke barked out a laugh of derision. "In case you haven't noticed, I'm not a politician. Just a businessman."

"We both know you are more than a businessman. And you have a lot of influence. Some men do what you say and will follow you and die for you."

"All this is inconsequential if I'm dead anyway."

Ebuka sighed. "I think I know how to keep you alive. I just needed to know for myself if you're capable of keeping your father's legacy alive."

"And are you satisfied?"

"I think you'll do the right thing when the time comes."

"I still don't understand your stake in all this. How did you find out about the plot against me?"

He shifted in his seat, looking uncomfortable for the first time since they started chatting.

"I know the person who has been contracted to kill you."

The faint pop distracted Duke from his words. The noise was too familiar to ignore. He raised his left hand, indicating for Ebuka to be quiet.

A glance through the window showed Mason was on the phone. The door at the back of the café squeaked, and someone entered the restaurant.

Duke pushed off the seat with one hand on the table, the other reached for his handgun and pointed it at Ebuka's head.

"Stand up. Keep your hands on your head. No sudden movement," he said, keeping his voice low and urgent.

"What's going on?" Ebuka stood and raised his arms in compliance.

Duke walked behind him and pulled a zip wire from his pocket. "I should be asking you. Slowly lower your hands to the back and keep them together."

Ebuka didn't argue as Duke tied his wrists together, making sure it was tight.

"Why are you doing this?" he asked, sounding worried, and his eyebrows drew together.

Duke pressed the dial button to call Mason but didn't lift the phone. "Your friend is here."

Ebuka gasped, his head jerking back, just as a woman walked into the main room of the café.

"Yes, I am," the woman spoke, her voice low. She wore skinny black trousers, a black polo neck shirt, and grey sneakers that seemed to match her eye colour. Her eyes were sharp and cold and hard as steel. In her gloved right hand was a black gun with a silencer nozzle.

Duke recognised an angel of death. A killer.

Xandra Gowon. Assassin for hire. Affiliated with the Himba cabal headed by Tiye Himba who controlled the middle belt region.

Duke hadn't met her before, but her deadly reputation preceded her. Everyone who'd ever been on her hit list had met their demise one way or the other. Things were not looking great for Duke, considering he'd made it onto Xandra's list.

His heart felt like it would explode out of his chest and sweat beaded on his upper lip. He stood, back to the wall, with Ebuka providing a human barrier. The newcomer stood closer to the exit, blocking his escape route.

On the upside, Mason, Maddox and team were still out there.

"Xan..." Ebuka licked his lips. "What are you doing here?"

"I came to kill two birds with one stone." Xandra's gaze went to Ebuka although she didn't move from the spot.

"What do you mean by that?"

"I find out that my lover has betrayed me, and there's only one way this can end. And Mr Odili—" She tilted her head in his direction, "—was already on the list. You only accelerated my plans on his account."

"No." Ebuka took a step in her direction.

"Stay where you are." Duke held the man with one hand, not willing to relinquish the flimsy barrier.

Ebuka glanced back. "Let me talk to her. I can sort this out."

"You mean you want to convince her not to kill you. It's not going to stop her from trying to kill me, even if you resolve your lovers' quarrel."

Ebuka's eyes narrowed. "Look—"

"Yeah, exactly how do you plan on changing my mind?" Xandra crossed her arms over her chest, her gun pointing away, her legs spread out. "You fucking betrayed me."

"No. I didn't betray you, Xan, and Mr Odili here is not your enemy," Ebuka pleaded.

Xandra rolled her eyes in derision.

Duke coughed.

Ebuka eyeballed him in a 'shut up' manner. He turned back to Ms Gowon. "I came here to negotiate a deal between the two of you. I think the two of you can work together. In fact, I believe Mr Odili is in the market for a new assassin."

Duke was going to comment, but a glance from Ebuka made him keep quiet. It looked as though his words were having an impact on Xandra. For one thing, the weapon wasn't pointed at Duke, and her attention focused on Ebuka, which gave Duke time to send a message to his men. He pressed the button on his phone to link with Maddox and lifted it to his ears.

"Boss, I have her in my crosshairs. What do you want me to do?"

Duke expelled air that had built up in his lungs when he saw the red dot on Xandra's chest. "Wait."

Ebuka's body froze. He'd spotted the mark, too. "No. Duke, tell your men to stand down."

"Tell your woman to stand down first," Duke replied. "Weapons on the floor."

"Xan, do as he says."

Xandra eyed him and then looked down to find the spot on her chest. She stared at Duke. "Well played, Mr Odili. I was told you were a hard man to kill. But I didn't think you would use my lover as a weapon to keep me distracted. It seems someone dies today, after all."

"If I'd wanted you dead, I would've given the order already," Duke said.

"So, what do you want from me?" she asked as the weapon clattered onto the linoleum floor.

Mason pushed in the front door with the ding of the bell and stepped in, gun pointing at Xandra. But he didn't say anything, just picked up the discarded pistol from the floor and tucked it into the back of his trousers.

"I think that Mr Njoku makes some valid points," Duke said, lowering his weapon, so it pointed downward. He couldn't relax. This was a very highly skilled hitwoman who had killed people without a gun before. "I'm in the market for good people, and you two seem like good people to me."

Xandra laughed, but it was dry and without humour. "You want me to come and work for you. I already have an employer who wouldn't be too pleased with that proposition."

"Yes. Tiye Himba is a tough bastard. What do you think will happen when he finds out about you two? You'll both be food for the fishes, that's what."

"Are you saying that you'll be a different kind of boss?" Ebuka asked.

"I give you my word that the two of you won't be harassed about your relationship if you come to work for me."

"You're offering me a job, as well?" Ebuka asked. "I don't know much about your business."

"As long as you're willing to do whatever is required, there's not much to it." Duke shrugged. "You'll both have my protection."

He nodded before turning to the assassin.

"Let's do this." He seemed to be imploring.

"You do realise that would mean that I'll become a target. Tiye Himba won't be happy about this."

"Yeah, you're right." Ebuka nodded.

"But on the other hand, this hit wasn't contracted by him. The contract is with John Bull Owo." Xandra walked over and leaned against the counter next to Ebuka. Mason and Duke exchanged glances but didn't say anything.

"And I don't owe The Baron any allegiances. So, I couldn't care less if he's pissed off," she continued, smiling for the first time.

Ebuka chuckled.

"Do we have a deal?" Duke asked.

"Yes," Ebuka said.

Xandra nodded. "You sure do."

She came close, offering her hand and Duke shook it. Ebuka stepped forward. Duke indicated for Mason to cut the tie binding his hands. Mason came across and introduced himself as he released Ebuka.

Duke exhaled a sigh of relief. He'd live for another day.

# TWENTY-FOUR

ON THE way home, Duke called each of his capos and invited them for an emergency meeting. Then he spent the next hours in conference with them, completing the plan they'd started a few days ago after the failed abduction attempt.

The plan to take down The Baron.

His phone buzzed. The clock on the screen read as 00:16 hours. He picked up the cell and swiped the screen.

*Is the meeting ending soon?* He read the message from Carla.

Duke's hand had a slight shake as he returned the phone to the table. He closed his eyes, briefly letting out a sigh.

He hadn't seen Carla since he left home that afternoon. He needed to see her if only for a little while. This meeting wouldn't be ending soon, and he didn't want to wait until who knew when. Now was a good time to take a break.

"Gentlemen, let's take fifteen minutes. There are refreshments in the kitchen."

The men murmured and nodded.

Duke left the den and headed upstairs to the bedrooms. Pushing open the door to his room, he called out, "Carla."

He checked the bathroom and walk-in closet. Still no Carla. "Where are you?"

Then he headed to her old room which she used as a walk-in closet. The door was slightly ajar. She was humming to a song and swinging her hips as she danced while folding laundry.

Duke stood there watching her for a few seconds as she swayed obliviously to the track via her headphones of the music player.

Drifting conversation from downstairs reminded him about the limited time. He walked into the room and wrapped his arms around her from behind.

She twisted her head, and a beautiful smile lit up her face as she pulled the headphones off. "I thought you were in a meeting."

"I was. I wanted to see you." He stroked up her body from belly to breast.

"You missed me." Her eyes twinkled, and her lips curled in a teasing smile.

"I did."

Her gripped her kinky hair, tilted her head and kissed her. Hard and slow, he savoured her taste. She gave a needy moan, and her free hand came around to grip Duke's hip.

He needed little stimulation to get aroused with Carla. The sound of her need for him was enough to make him hard and throbbing, the weight of his erection pushing the trousers and resting against her left butt cheek. And if he wanted to bend her over the mattress and fuck her, she would let him without hesitation.

But Duke wanted to wait, to take his time. So, he pressed in hard with his mouth and hip for a few more seconds and let her go.

"I need to get back to the meeting shortly."

"Okay." She twisted in his arms, lips in a pout. "Do you know how long you'll be?"

"I'm not sure. Probably another couple of hours. We need to arrange to move your things into my closet. You share my bed, so you might as well share my closet."

"Sure." She smiled. "You're the boss."

"That, I am."

Duke gave her a quick kiss and stepped back. "No need to wait up for me. I'll wake you when I finish."

"I hope so," she said and winked at me.

The smile remained on Duke's face as he descended the stairs and headed first to the kitchen for some caffeine.

They went back to the meeting, and by the time he got to his room, the sun was on its way up.

Carla sat up in bed with a personal tablet device in her hands.

"You're up already?" Duke asked as he stripped off his clothes.

"I couldn't sleep so I decided to watch a movie."

"Give me five, and I'll be with you."

Naked, he walked into the en-suite bathroom, had a quick shower, towelled off, and was back in the bedroom as fast as he could.

He pulled off the sheet covering Carla to reveal her naked body. His Cara was gloriously beautiful with smooth, soft skin. He loved that she kept her body hairless. The only exceptions were the narrow strip on her labia and the mass of curly brown hair on her head that he loved tangling his fingers in and tugging her head back.

Starting from her feet, he kissed inches of skin slowly as he travelled up. He kissed her hips but didn't touch her pussy. Her clit was swollen, peaking out and glistening.

He loved the taste of her, the feel of her. He could never get enough of her.

She writhed and moaned, but he ignored her and continued the slow torture of her body, paying attention to her navel. At her breasts, he worried one with his teeth while he squeezed and pinched the other. She wriggled and moaned and started begging.

"Please, Bae...Fuck... Please fuck me." Tears beaded her lashes.

Her plea was enough to put him on edge. He couldn't wait any longer. "Pass me the lube."

She loved using the special lube that made her extra sensitive and tingly inside and out. She fumbled to open the drawer before pulling out the tube and uncapping it. He squeezed some onto his hand and smeared his dick. He reached for her, but she spread her legs.

"I'm ready. Please."

Sure enough, his fingers slid into her slit without much resistance. "You prepped for me."

Moving restlessly, she lowered her lashes in a shy smile. "Yes. I knew you'd need me after your meeting."

Grinning, Duke shifted between her legs and pressed against her. With a thrust, he was buried inside her slick channel. Hot as a furnace, she swallowed him, and for a moment, he didn't want to move.

"Oh," he groaned. "You feel so good. So perfect."

Tilting his head back, he gripped her hips, trying not to lose it before he'd even started. After a few shallow breaths, he lowered his body over her and started moving, a slow thrust in and a long slide out, grinding their hips in-between.

She mewled and melted; her body pliant as she clung onto his back.

"You are so magnificent when you're like this," she said.

Surprised, he paused for a beat before stroking in. "Like how?"

"Like this. Dominant and unguarded, all at the same time. I've never met anyone who could combine both qualities and still be true to themselves. It's partly why I love you."

Her declaration left him speechless, and his chest tightened. With everything going on, could he live up to her love? Could he keep her and protect her?

His chest tightened each time he thought about her.

He loved her. But he couldn't bring himself to say it, afraid he would jinx everything.

The last time he told someone he loved them, they wounded up dead. His parents' death had stopped him from using those words again.

Pushing the heavy thoughts aside, he kissed Carla, injecting all the emotions he felt for her into the kiss. There was no reason he couldn't show how he felt about her. He traced lips along her smooth chin, nipping the skin from there to her collarbone.

Her writhing increased as her pussy gripped him. He continued the leisurely lovemaking, building their pleasures until his body demanded release. Increasing the pace, he began slamming in and out, again and again, while playing with her swollen clit.

"Oh ... Oh ... Oh ... Duke."

She disintegrated in an orgasm, singing his name beautifully as she undulated and contracted inside and out.

His body hummed with want, his balls aching. Settling on his knees, he rammed into her, the thrusts arrhythmic as his body took over, focused only on pleasure. He buried himself inside her and came, body shuddering so many times, and he collapsed on top of her.

She wrapped her arms around him, hugging him tight while her lips brushed his sweaty forehead.

He couldn't speak for a few seconds; the only sounds were of their breathing and slowing heart rates.

"You're going to kill my father, aren't you?" Carla said when the silence stretched.

Duke didn't answer, not knowing what to say. Her father was merciless. Did she want to know that her lover was the same kind of man?

"Please find another way. Don't kill him. Please. I couldn't live with his death on my mind, too."

Slipping out of her, Duke leaned up and brushed his lips against her forehead, but she pushed him back.

"Promise me," she said, meeting his gaze.

"I'm going to take your father's organisation down and destroy it," he said finally, keeping his gaze so she could understand the severity of his words. "But I won't kill him."

Blowing out a deep breath, she pulled him down and brushed her lips against his. "Thank you."

# TWENTY-FIVE

JOHN BULL Owo didn't plan to get married again. But nothing gave him as much pleasure as the company of a woman. He kept several mistresses all over the city, preferring to visit the women at irregular intervals so that there wasn't a pattern to his movement, making it difficult for any planned attacks.

So, when an unplanned visit to one of the said mistresses revealed she was seriously unwell and in hospital, he'd simply redirected his convoy to the nearest available mistress.

Gabriela was a pretty, big-busted girl with long dark hair and legs from here to next Sunday. She was his newest mistress. She'd been at a party he'd attended about two weeks ago. She'd given him an amazing blowjob, so he'd decided to set her up as one of his girls in one of his apartments.

He always installed the women in his properties. He had several across the city. This way, he had access to the building, and he could turn up unannounced. Also, if the women ever misbehaved, he could get rid of them and install others.

Of course, he could invite the women to come to his house instead and save himself the hassle of travelling out to meet them. But he hated having women in the house. He'd done that in the early days after the death of his wife. But each woman he'd brought to the house had assumed they were going to be the next Mrs Owo by making demands on him. He'd quickly divested them of that notion. He would never trust a woman enough again to make her his wife.

One girl was unavailable this afternoon, he didn't want to risk that another one would be the same, so he rang ahead. Gabriela confirmed that she was home and would be ready for him.

He relaxed back into the seat of the blacked-out SUV, another one of the same colour following behind.

Thirty minutes later, they pulled into the arching driveway outside a colonial-style building set on four levels with terracotta and cream walls and balconies for each apartment.

His men jumped out of the cars to secure the location, and one opened the door for him. He stepped out.

Boom! The second SUV flew ten feet into the air and smashed to the ground in an explosion.

John Bull hit the tarmac in a crouch as gunshots zinged around him. One of his bodyguards, Gbenga, dragged him up as he pulled out his weapon.

"Get in," he ordered the men into the car as he climbed back in.

The driver, Ade, gunned the engine toward the exit only to see it blocked by two SUVs. Bullets hit the car, not piercing it. The vehicle was bullet-proof, but the security of the enclosed place didn't cheer him. Not if there was another rocket-propelled grenade out there.

"Back up," he shouted. The only safe place was the building since the shots were coming from the driveway and the road.

The driver reversed the car, the wheels squealing. With a jerk, it stopped in front of the building entrance.

John Bull pushed the door open and rushed out toward the building entrance. Ade and Gbenga covered his back as he raced up the stairs. His hand shook as he punched the code for the door.

There was a pop, and he shoved the slab and stepped into the bright corridor. He ran all the way to the top floor, the two men from the lead car right behind him.

For his middle age, he was still relatively fit. He swam every day, played tennis twice a week, and rode horses for polo tournaments during the season.

A sheen of sweat broke on his skin at he banged his fist on the door to Gabriela's apartment. The door opened, and he didn't even look at the woman who greeted him.

"Are you okay, JB?" she asked. "What's going on?"

He shoved past her into the hallway. "No. I'm not. Some fucker is trying to kill me. Stay out of my way."

The woman gasped as he entered the tastefully decorated living room. The sounds of gunfire from downstairs reached here. He still had men downstairs fighting. There had been six in the convoy; two in the car with him and four in the second car.

Ade stood by the entrance, and Gbenga went to the window, tugged the curtain aside, and peered outside.

"What's happening?" John Bull asked.

"We're down two men, sir," Gbenga replied. "And there seems to be eight men advancing on the building."

"Fuck!" John Bull kicked the table and paced the space. He was fucked if he didn't get more men. Gun in one hand and phone in the other, he called Marlon.

"Hey, Dad," his son greeted. "What's up?"

"I need more men. I'm under attack."

"What? Where?"

"In Elizabeth Garden City. Some son of a bitch wants to mess with me. I'll show them why I'm called The Baron. Send the men immediately."

"Of course, Dad. I'm on my way."

John Bull switched off his phone and shoved it back in his pocket. "You two go out there and secure the building. We have reinforcements on the way."

"Yes, Boss."

The two men walked out, leaving John Bull to his churning thoughts.

Who the fuck was trying to kill him? Of course, he knew he had plenty of people who wanted him dead, putting aside the obvious ones like Duke Odili. But Mr Odili didn't have the balls to pull off something like this. In all the years he'd squared off to the man, he'd never pulled anything like this.

This seemed more like something rivals trying to muscle into his territory would do. And the glimpses of the men he'd seen, they had balaclavas over their heads so he couldn't tell one way or the other.

"Fuck!" That's what he'd rather be doing than dealing with those bastards out there. "Gabriela! Get me a drink."

He sat on the sofa and placed his gun on the table. Gabriela returned with a bottle of Tequila and a glass with some already poured in. Her hand shook as she put them on the table. His gaze scanned her body. She really was pretty in her V-neck blue dress that flared at the bottom. He would fuck her once this was sorted.

He took the glass and tossed the drink into his throat. The kick of pepper, spice, and fruit burned the back of his mouth. He slammed the glass on the table and poured another shot, but his hand shook as he returned the bottle to the table. His vision blurred, Gabriela fading in and out.

The bitch had drugged him. He reached for his gun, raised it, and fired a shot in her direction before he slumped on the sofa, blacked out.

****

John Bull woke to bright light that hurt his eyes, and he squinted as he tried to take in his environment. He sat bound to a rusty metal chair, his hands behind his back. Trash littered the concrete floor.

Men stood around in what seemed to be an abandoned warehouse. One of them approached him. His mouth fell open when he recognised the dark-haired man.

"Welcome back, Mr Owo," his daughter's lover said in a hard voice.

"I'm going to kill you, Odili." John Bull spat on the floor, jerking his body with the chair.

He wanted to reach out and choke the man with his hands. He couldn't believe the ọmọkunrin Igbo had pulled this off. Hadn't thought the man was brave enough.

The man stepped closer, bearing over him. "You're not in a position to kill anyone. See, we're going to play a game where I ask questions, and you answer them. At the end of it all, we're going to have a deal between you and me. Do you understand?"

"Over my dead body!" He'd gambled that Mr Odili didn't want him dead; otherwise, he would've been already. If the reverse had been the case, he would've killed the man.

"Well, that can be arranged." Duke stepped back, and two of the other men came forward.

They laid into him, fists connecting with his chest and face. Pain ricocheted through him. He took most of it with grunts. But it became unbearable, and he cried out for them to stop.

Duke raised his hand, and the men stopped.

John Bull spluttered, coughing out blood as his ribs hurt. His face felt swollen, and he imagined it would be covered in bruises.

"Let's try that again," Mr Odili said as he stepped close.

John Bull eyed the man, realising he had a new respect for him. He had no tolerance for weak people, which had been part of his annoyance with his daughter Carla who had the gentle constitution of her mother. In his business, vulnerable people were eaten up. They never survived. But perhaps with Mr Odili in Carla's life, the girl would grow a backbone.

"What do you want to know?" he asked, his throat dry and hurting.

The other man pulled up another rusty chair and straddled it, facing John Bull. "I've been investigating the deaths of my parents, and your name came up. I believe you can tell me what happened to them."

JB sneered as the memories of what he'd done years ago came rushing back. He'd been young and eager to rise to the top. He'd climbed the crime ladder very quickly, going from foot soldier to capo in little time. But he'd wanted to be the boss. So, he'd set up a side-line, siphoning off from his boss and setting up his own cocaine factory. Then his boss had given him an assignment.

A statesman was making waves with the legislators. The people loved him, and he was the favourite runner for the next president.

"Your father's opponents didn't want him to be president. You see, he was extremely popular with the people. Many felt he was going to put them out of business and tighten law enforcement to bring it back under the state. We took him out."

Odili's body tensed as if he were restraining himself. "What did you do?"

John Bull lifted his shoulders and winced. "We knew he was on holiday. But the risks associated with getting away there were higher. So, we had to lure him back to the city via his secretary. I was in the team that stormed your home. We took out the security team, shot your father in his office, and found your mother in her bedroom. I enjoyed slitting her throat."

John Bull laughed.

Duke jumped up, picked up the chair, and flung it at the wall. It clattered loudly. He tipped his head back and growled furiously, his hands bunched into fists by his sides. Then he strolled to a table in the corner and lifted a battery-powered hand drill from the table. He turned it on, and the whirring sound filled the air, causing John Bull's shoulder to tighten and his legs to shake.

"Get out," Duke shouted.

The men stood still, seemingly shocked by his outburst. One of them approached him and said something in a low voice John Bull didn't catch.

"I said, get out. All of you!"

The men lifted their hands and strolled out of the door in the far end.

Duke inserted a drill bit to the machine and came over and leaned over him.

"Before I came on this mission, your daughter Carla made me promise to keep you alive. And because I love her, I made her that promise. But listening to you talk about killing my parents without one ounce of remorse in you, I know you don't deserve to live. I know you won't stop coming after me until I wind up dead. And I can't let that happen. This ends tonight."

The tool in Duke's hand whirred again as the bit drilled through the fabric of his trousers into the flesh on John Bull's left thigh. Excruciating pain seared through him and his terrified scream filled the cavernous space, rebounding off the walls a thousand times.

# TWENTY-SIX

CARLA HADN'T seen Duke in a week. The only contact with him had been a brief conversation followed by phone sex where they'd watched each other masturbate on screen.

Duke had said he needed to be in communications blackout so that their actions and locations would not be tracked.

Every day she worried about him, praying he would come home safely. She'd never known she would miss anyone the way she missed him.

This morning, she woke with a sick feeling in her stomach. After dressing, she stepped out to the balcony and glanced down at the lobby below.

No one was there.

Strange. Jide or one of the other bodyguards usually waited there.

She hurried down the stairs and into the sitting room where Jide and Lebechi sat on sofas.

"Carla, you're awake." Jide switched off the TV which had been on a news channel.

"Have you heard from Duke?" She flopped on the sofa and grabbed the remote.

"No." He took the remote from her. "Come on. Let me get you breakfast."

He was acting strange. He didn't usually get her meals.

"I'm not hungry. Can I have the remote back?" She extended her hand.

"Nothing is interesting on TV. Let's go outside."

This was ridiculous. "I don't want to go outside. What's going on?"

"Nothing."

"Then give me the controller."

He puffed out a breath and passed the gadget over.

She flicked the TV on.

The news channel had breaking news announcing the death of John Bull Owo in a car bomb. Assassinated in a cartel war.

The remote slipped from her hand, and she slumped on the sofa.

Her father was dead? A car bomb?

Images of Daddy flashed in her head. Of the last time she'd seen him.

She might not have liked her father. But she didn't hate him. She would never have wished for him to die this way.

"I'm sorry," Jide said, placing his hand on her shoulder.

Duke had killed her father. The man she loved was a callous killer, exactly like her father. She couldn't live with him.

Tears stinging the back of her eyes, she turned to Jide. "I need a phone."

"It's on the table." Jide picked it. "What are you going to do?"

"I'm going home," she said, meeting his gaze.

He frowned. "Are you sure that's wise?"

"I'm sure. I have no reason to be here any longer. The threat against Duke has been nullified."

He nodded and handed her the phone. She called her brother.

"Marlon," she said when he answered, her voice scratchy. "I want to come home."

"I'll make the arrangement. Get to the airport. You'll have a seat on any flight to Lori Osa."

"Okay. Thank you."

She handed the phone back to Jide. "I need to get to the airport."

"I'll have to clear with the boss first."

"Do whatever you have to do. Just get me out of here."

She walked out and went to the bedroom to pack but realised when she got there that she didn't have any belongings in this house. She'd left home with only the clothes on her back, phone, wallet, and sunglasses. She knew where Duke kept the items, so she grabbed them before heading out.

Jide met her outside the house. "Boss says I should drive you to the airport."

Pain cut across her chest. Duke was letting her go. He'd sworn he'd never let her go. Then again, he'd sworn he wouldn't kill her father.

She would never trust anything he said again.

She slid the sunglasses over her face to cover the pain in her eyes. Jide drove her to the airport. When she got to the check-in counter, the girl confirmed she was on the flight.

She said goodbye to Jide. She would miss him. He'd been kind to her.

On the flight, she drowned her sorrow in the alcohol offered. Bola picked her up at the Lori Osa terminal.

"I'm sorry about your father," he said.

"Thank you." She gave him a short nod.

They drove home in silence. The house was noticeably quiet, and she went in search of Dupe first. The minute she saw the old woman, she couldn't hold back anymore and broke down in tears. Dupe hugged Carla until she calmed down.

"You're going to have to be strong, my dear."

She swiped her eyes and nodded. "Where is Marlon?"

"He's in your father's den. He didn't waste any time installing himself in your father's place. Be careful with him. That boy has so much darkness in him."

"I better go and pay my respect to the new baron."

Dupe rolled her eyes upward but waved her on. She headed to her father's office and knocked on the door.

"Come in," her brother said.

She pushed the door open, a little disorientated when she walked in and didn't see her father at his desk. Instead, her brother sat there, one of the bodyguards standing behind him. He wasn't Daddy, no matter how much he wished he was.

He stood and gave her a brief hug, which surprised her.  Her brother had been barely cordial when she lived here.

"It's good that you finally saw sense instead of cavorting with the enemy."

"I learnt my lesson."

"Good. Welcome home. You can go and relax. I'm sure you must be exhausted. When you've freshened up, we can have dinner."

She nodded and headed to the door before turning back. "When is the funeral?"

"It's scheduled for Saturday."

She swallowed. "Let me know what I need to do."

"Of course. We'll discuss it at dinner."

She went to her room, glad to be back in it but feeling detached, like it wasn't hers anymore. She showered and got dressed. Exhaustion weighed on her limbs. But she had to have dinner with Marlon before she could sleep, so she headed to the dining room.

Marlon already sat at the table. They discussed the funeral arrangements while eating. She opted to drink water since she had so much alcohol on the flight, but he offered her a glass of red wine, which she took.

"Once the funeral is over, you will be marrying Abdul. It has all been arranged," her brother announced.

"I'll do whatever you want me to do." Carla didn't argue. She didn't care anymore. Her heart was broken—shattered—by the man she loved. Her brother was only being himself. It was in his nature to be cruel.

Feeling overwhelmed, she stood, intending to head to bed. She took two steps and collapsed.

***

Duke was still in Lori Osa when news of John Bull's death broke. Of course, they'd needed to concentrate on getting out of there alive, so he hadn't been thinking straight when Jide had called to ask if Carla could go home.

He hadn't wanted his beloved gone. But it would have been unfair to keep her in Opal City when she needed to grieve for her father.

Coming home to no Carla had been agonising, made worse by the fact she didn't call him. When Duke called her house, he was told she was unavailable.

By the end of the week, Duke's mood didn't improve. He walked into the kitchen to find Mason there. He shut the door. His head was lowered, and his shoulders slumped. In his hand was his gun.

"What's going on?" Duke asked, striding over to the fridge.

"I should be asking you that," he said, his expression stony.

"Hmmm?" Duke didn't get his mood. He had other things on his mind. Like Carla. "Did something happen?"

"It's you I'm worried about."

"You're worried about me? Why?" He turned away to grab a bottle of water and a glass. Survival instincts dictated he shouldn't turn his back to a man holding a gun. But this was Mason. His capo, best friend and the closest person to him. A brother

"Duke, sit down."

The warning in his deep voice made Duke tilt his head to look at him. His stiff shoulders, high chin and tight expression showed he was angry, as much as the gun now pointed in Duke's direction.

"What the fuck, Mace—"

"Sit the fuck down, Duke, or I swear I won't be responsible."

If this had been anyone else, Duke would've challenged them. But he'd never seen Mason's anger directed at him in this manner before. Or him pointing a gun at Duke's head ever.

"Fine." Raising both hands in an unthreatening manner. Duke walked over, pulled out a tall stool by the breakfast table and lowered his body onto it. He rested one elbow on the tabletop and settled the other hand on his thigh. "What's this about?"

"You. This is about you. You've been like shit all week." He puffed out a heavy breath and stepped forward, gun still levelled. "What's going on between you and Carla?"

Duke's heart thudded loud and fast. This was the moment of reckoning. He knew it would come one day. But not now. He wanted to see Carla again before he joined his ancestors in the great beyond.

"Are you going to kill me?"

He shook his head slowly as if disappointed by Duke's response. "You don't fucking do this. I've had your back for years. I've never questioned your choices or who you choose to fuck. But when you start doing things that jeopardise our family, the least you can do is respect me enough to tell me what's going on."

Duke heaved a sigh and scrubbed his face. He was right. Duke trusted Mason to watch his back, yet he hadn't revealed the most crucial thing in life to the man. His love for Carla.

"I never, ever want to disrespect you, Mason. Everything aside, you're my best friend."

"Then tell me the truth about Carla."

Nodding, Duke blurted it all out. "I'm in love with the woman, and I want her in my life. But you know this will cause problems now that The Baron is eliminated, and there is no longer a need for a truce between the two families."

"True." Mason nodded, pulled out another chair and sat down, his gun on the table. "Some might take you for a weakling. Although after your takedown of The Baron, not many will openly challenge you."

He scratched the stubble on his chin. "But there are a few men who will always have your back. Me, for one. Jide. Maddox. Then, of course, you now have Ebuka Njoku and Xandra Gowon, too."

Duke puffed out the breath he'd been holding. Knowing Mason wouldn't put a bullet through him was a welcome relief. He capitalised on the opportunity. "I want her back, Mace. I'm going nuts in here without her."

Mason grinned, showing white teeth. "Then what are we waiting for? Let's go and get your woman back."

***

Duke arrived at Carla's house in the convoy of mourners returning from the cemetery where John Bull Owo had been buried. He'd been there, watching Carla as her father had been laid to rest. She'd worn oversized sunshades that eclipsed her face. But he didn't miss the bowed head, tight lips and crumpled shoulders. He'd wanted to go to her.

Now, the security at the gates let them in without trouble. He wasn't expecting trouble. This was a day of mourning.

"Wait in the car. I won't be long," Duke said.

"Are you sure?" Mason frowned. "I don't trust Marlon."

"Neither do I. But I want to get Carla out without incident, and having more than one of us in there will attract attention."

"Still, if you're not out in thirty minutes, I'm coming in."

"Fair enough."

In the house, people stood or sat in groups, nibbling on refreshments and talking in low voices. He took the steps up to the mezzanine level.

She stood beside the pool, looking forlorn and alone.

Wishing he could shield her from this grief, the back of his throat hurt. He twisted the door handle, intent on going to her and giving as much comfort as she needed.

From the corner of his eye, he noticed a shadow but did not move in time to avoid the stun gun. His body spasmed, and he tumbled onto the marble floor.

Two men dragged him into a room and strapped him into a chair, taking turns to hit him.

"You are bold. I'll give you that." Marlon stood before him, gun in hand. "But you must also be out of your mind to think you can walk in here in broad daylight and nothing will happen to you."

"I came to get my wife," Duke said and spat out blood.

"Your wife?" Abdul Sani, who had been standing behind Marlon, stepped forward.

"Didn't she tell you? We took our vows two weeks ago." Duke curled his split, hurting lips in a grin, knowing how that would piss off the man.

"Did you know that?" Abdul turned his rage on Marlon. "Are you trying to double-cross me? Our deal won't work if she's married to someone else."

"Calm the fuck down, will you." Marlon snapped. "He's talking nonsense. Carla is not married to him. I would know."

"Would you?" Duke mocked.

"Shut the fuck up." Marlon smacked him across the face.

Duke moved his aching jaw. "I'm just saying. Carla can't get married to anyone else without renouncing her vows to me."

"I want to talk to her." Abdul started towards the door.

Marlon stopped him with a hand on the shoulder. "Hold on. Do you actually believe him?"

"There's nothing wrong with getting a confirmation from her."

"Fine." Marlon turned to another man. "Bring my sister here."

The man yanked the door open, and everyone stared at Carla. It seemed she'd been standing outside the door all along.

"I'm right here." She sashayed into the room, swaying on her feet. She wore a black skirt suit and black pumps.

Duke's heart warmed at seeing her so close. But something was off about her.

Was she drunk?

She slumped into a sofa and looked at him, pupils dilated. She sniffed and turned away.

Damn it. She was high.

"Carla, what did you take?" he asked in a sharp tone.

"It's none of your business," she shouted.

"You're my wife!" He allowed his anger to seep through. Jerking to get out of the chair.

"Is that true?" Abdul cut in. "Are you married to him?"

"Stay out of this." Duke tugged at his bonds again, trying to loosen them.

"I want to know the truth." Abdul yanked Carla from her seat.

Duke growled his anger. He was going to kill Abdul if he hurt her.

"Yes. Duke and I got married. But I want a divorce." She yanked away from Abdul and grabbed Marlon's gun, stalking towards Duke.

Shock smashed through Duke. "You want a divorce? Why?"

Was it just the drugs making her say nasty things to him?

She pointed the gun at his head. "You know why."

His heart was beating fast, and sweat dripped down his face. He wanted to believe that she wouldn't shoot him. But she was also high on drugs, probably blow, which made her unpredictable.

"Listen to me, Carla. I won't give you a divorce. You're my wife."

"Then I'll become your widow." She released the safety on the weapon and pointed it back at him.

"Fine. If you want to kill me, first tell me why."

She sniffed and shook her head. Tears pooled in her eyes when she looked at him again. "You promised you wouldn't kill my father. Yet you killed him."

"Carla, listen to me. I didn't kill your father."

"Liar!" she screeched.

A bullet whizzed past his face and embedded in the wall behind him with a bang.

His heart nearly crashed through his chest. The woman he knew would never kill another person. The drugs were making her reckless and paranoid. "Carla!"

"What? Do you think I won't shoot you? I am an Owo. Have you forgotten?"

"I know who you are, Carla. I know you don't want to do this."

"You don't know jack about me. This is me. You killed the other Carla when you killed Daddy."

"Damn it, Carla. I didn't kill your father."

She wavered and tilted her head to study him.

He continued, hoping to get through the drug-fuelled blood lust in her mind. "I swear to you, I did not kill your father. You know if I did, I would admit it. There's no reason to hide it from you. You know me."

"If you didn't, then who did?"

"Ask your brother."

"My brother?" She turned with a frown on her face. "Marlon, what is he talking about?"

"Don't listen to him. Shoot him," her brother replied.

"I want to know what he's talking about. Who killed Daddy?"

"Oh, for fuck sake. Give me the gun."

Carla jerked back and raised the gun in Marlon's direction. "No! I want an answer."

Marlon glared at her. "Yes. I killed Daddy. The old man was becoming soft. First, he allowed the man to disrespect him by walking into his house and take a hostage. Then he made a deal, allowing Duke to marry you."

"Daddy made a deal with Duke?" Carla sounded in shock.

"Yes. He was going to ruin everything. Now shoot the motherfucker or give me the fucking gun, so I can do it myself." Marlon grabbed the gun. Carla didn't let go, and a shot went off.

"Carla!" Duke shouted, fearing the worst.

Marlon froze, his eyes glazed over. "You shot me."

Then he staggered back and collapsed onto a sofa, clutching his stomach as blood seeping into his clothes.

Abdul reached for Carla.

"Back off!" She pointed the gun at Abdul.

Abdul raised his hand and said in an accusatory tone. "Carla, you shot your brother. He needs medical help."

"I don't care. Get the fuck out of my house," Carla said.

"What?"

"You heard me. Get out, or I'll shoot you. I've already shot my brother. I like you even less than I like him." She raised her brow.

"Fuck you, bitch!" Abdul glared at her before stomping out of the room.

"Bola, follow him and make sure he leaves."

The man left to obey her order. She turned to where her brother lay groaning.

"Carla?" Duke needed to be out of this chair.

She didn't turn to him. "Leke. Untie him"

The man pulled out a knife and sliced off the tapes from Duke's arms.

As soon as he was free, he ambled towards Carla and said in a soft voice. "It's okay, Cara."

He placed his palm on her arm, gently sliding down until he covered her hand. "Give me the gun."

She didn't resist when he unclasped her fingers from the trigger and took possession of the weapon. He slid the safety on, tucked the gun into his back strap and checked on Marlon.

He'd stopped breathing, and there was no pulse.

"Should we take him to a hospital?" Carla asked, sounding jittery.

Duke stood and shook his head. "I'm sorry. He's dead."

Carla let out a long wail and crumpled. He reached for her, catching her just before she hit the floor.

# TWENTY-SEVEN

DUKE WATCHED Carla sitting on the loveseat by the bay window overlooking the valley. For weeks, she'd been quiet, lost in her mind. His heart hurt at seeing her with the vacant stare in his eyes and shuffling steps. She seemed to have lost interest in life in general.

After the incident in her father's house resulting in Marlon's death, Duke had difficulty getting her out of Lori Osa. First, they'd had to deal with the police. Then there'd been the media furore. Through it all, Carla had barely said a word. He'd practically smuggled her out by private flight in the middle of the night.

Now Carla was in therapy. The doctor had reassured Duke that she was making improvement and would recover.

The healing process was slow because the incident had triggered memories of her mother's death, which compounded the trauma. Memories of John Bull pushing his wife down the stairs.

The back of Duke's throat hurt, and tears smarted his eyes. He had sworn to keep Carla safe, and he hadn't.

His phone beeped, pulling him out of his misery. He read the message from Sophie.

*Gabriela thanks you for her new home. It's beautiful.*

Gabriela was a friend of Sophie, who they'd planted at one of John Bull's clubs, hoping he'd take the bait, and he had. She had helped them to take him down.

Duke had relocated her into one of their safe houses for a few days. Now that John Bull and Marlon were dead, Sophie had found her a new home.

*Tell her 'she's welcome,' Duke replied.*

Another ping almost instantly. *How is Carla doing?*

He scrubbed a hand over his face as he stared at Carla again. He needed to regain his composure before going to her. She was jumpy anytime someone touched her or came close. So, she spent most of the time in isolation or with Duke.

Duke sent a quick reply to Sophie. *Not much change.*

He turned away and took a deep breath before striding across the room in her direction.

"Carla," he said in a low voice to prevent startling her.

She flinched and looked up. The corners of her lips curled into a little smile.

"How are you feeling today?" he asked, still standing.

"Okay." She shrugged.

"This view is beautiful. The lush green of the meadows, the crystal blue of the river, the white walls and red roofs of the village in the valley. I've been taking pictures on my phone." She lifted the gadget in his hand. "I want to get some turned into large prints and hang them up in the house."

"It's a nice view." Her words reminded Duke of the reason he wanted to talk to her. "Can I have a seat?"

He had to be careful to avoid triggering an episode with Carla. He had to hold back when he wanted to touch her or hug her and ask for permission first.

"Yes," she said, shifting to one end.

He settled beside her. The space wasn't massive. Their bodies touched, from thighs to arms, the closest he'd been to her in days. A rush of pleasure sent warmth spreading through him.

"Have you thought about what you want to do now?" he asked, hoping to reignite her love for life.

She glanced at him, her eyes glazed over. Blinking, she said, "I'd love to go back to film school and work on setting up my production company."

"Wonderful. Let me know what you need to make it happen. We can work it into our moving plan."

"Oh. Are you buying a new house?"

"I don't know what kind of property yet. I was hoping you'd choose it since it'll be our home, and it's in a city you know very well."

"I don't understand. You're letting me choose your home?"

"It's our home. You're my wife." Duke lowered his hand to her thigh, praying she wouldn't bolt. "You're the woman I love. I want us to share a home, a life, together."

It was the first time he'd told her how he truly felt. His hands trembled as he wondered how she would receive his words.

"You're serious," she shrieked, covering her mouth with her hand.

Her eyes were bright with unshed tears.

He wanted to pull her into his arms, to kiss her.

Then a tear dropped down her face, and she squeezed her eyes shut. "How can you love me after what I did?"

"What do you mean?"

Her body stiffened. She lowered her hand, turning her face away. "When my brother said I would still marry Abdul, I didn't fight him. After the first time he drugged me, I started taking more, seeking out whatever was on offer. I believed everything he said about you. I didn't care if I lived or died."

"Fuck! What?" Duke gripped her shoulders and tugged her to face him. He stared at her bowed head, unable to comprehend her motives.

She lifted her head, meeting his gaze. "I was heartbroken when I thought you'd killed Daddy. Then I go home only for my own brother to sell me out. What else was I going to live for?"

"You. You live for you. You're beautiful and fun and full of energy. Before you came into my life, I don't think I ever laughed so much. You care about the world and the people in it. You have so much to give."

She swiped her eyes. "Do you mean that?"

"Yes, never doubt my word. I know I'm not the easiest person to love, and I can't ever demand for you to do that. But I've never told you a lie, and I would never break my promises to you. That, you can always be certain."

"I realise that now. I'm sorry."

"No, I'm sorry. I didn't protect you. I left you alone and vulnerable while I went to chase for answers and deal with your father. I should've anticipated that your brother would try something devious. But I never thought he would kill his own father."

"I should've seen that coming. My brother had always been ambitious. He told me that Dad killed your parents. I'm sorry that all my family ever caused you is pain."

Duke squeezed her shoulder. He didn't care about her father or brother, only cared about her.

"I know about what your father did. He confessed it to me. But your brother and father aside, you are the best thing that ever happened to me. You're the balm that soothes my troubled soul. The only time I feel pain is when I see you hurting. I will do anything to see you smile again."

"Oh, Duke." She reached across and cupped his cheek, stroking the skin with her thumb. "I love you. Just love me back. That's all I want from you."

"That, I'll do for the rest of my life."

Thank you for reading PRINCE OF HEARTS by Kiru Taye.
If you enjoyed this book, please leave a review at the site of purchase.

Want to read an epilogue? Scan the QR code to receive bonus content.

For news about upcoming books in the Yadili series, sign up to receive Kiru's Newsletter on the website: www.kirutaye.com

 Continue reading for Chapter One from Xandra: Killer of Kings by Kiru Taye.

## YADILI SERIES (SO FAR)

Prince of Hearts (Duke & Carla)
Killer of Kings_(Xandra & Ebuka)
Bad Santa_(Osagie & Gina)
Rough Diamond (Mason & Sophie)
Tough Alliance_(Maddox & Zoe)

# KILLER OF KINGS – CHAPTER ONE

THE TARGET stepped out of the car. The door was held open by one of the bodyguards while the other stood by the front door of the white two-storey mansion.

The glow from the floor-level spotlights accentuated the deep lines on the man's umber-hued face, making him appear older than in the photograph. His gaze swept along the driveway as if he sensed something out of place.

Back pressed against the rough wall, Xandra remained frozen where the shadows swallowed her in the alcove between the brick perimeter fence and the hibiscus hedge. She wore nothing that would reflect the light—dark clothes, a hood over her head and a mask shielding her face. The morning was wet, cold, and dark, dawn still a few hours away. Her gaze stayed on him as she mentally confirmed he was the man she wanted.

Dimi Yahya. Forty-nine years old. Six feet tall. Eighty-five kilos. Grey hair grew at the sides of his neatly cut, short dark hair. His facial hair was shaved off, although a shadow showed on his chin. He dressed in an expensive, opaque, fitted suit that would've been made especially for him and his polished shoes shone under the streetlamp.

From this distance, his eye colour wasn't visible, but it would be brown—she'd seen it in the photograph sent over with his file.

Yahya walked down the narrow path.

Xandra waited. The car door obscured her line of fire.

The bodyguard shut it, giving her an opening.

She squeezed the trigger of the FN Five-seveN with a smooth, even pressure.

Fat drops of rain splattered on the pavement masking the *p-taff p-taff* of the suppressed gunshots. The man slumped against the side of the car with a dull thud, hit twice in the sternum in rapid succession.

The bodyguard by the front door let out a low curse as he spotted his colleague falling and ran towards Yahya, hand reaching inside his jacket.

Xandra squeezed out another couple of rounds of low-powered, subsonic 5.7mm bullets. The copper-enclosed lead tore through the skin of his back and neck. He collapsed forward, hitting the ground with a muted *thunk*, arm outstretched toward his boss.

Yahya froze in a crouch behind the car, eyes sweeping the area as he pulled out his handgun and held it ready to shoot. "Who are you? Be a man. Show yourself!"

Melting out of the darkness, Xandra took a measured step forward.

Yahya's eyes widened as soon as he saw her. It seemed he recognised her. That would be impossible considering she was covered from head to toes.

He understood her purpose, though—his death—and straightened confidently, the rain plastering wet clothes to his body.

"I'll pay you double—no—triple whatever he's paying you to kill me," he offered.

Her response was to squeeze the trigger of the FN Five-seveN in her hand and put a bullet through Yahya. He collapsed to his knees, a hole in his chest, right of his breastbone. She fired another shot into his head, right between the eyes just to be sure. In this job, there was no room for mistakes.

The expended cartridges clinked on the stones and rolled into a forming puddle shimmering with dull orange light.

He fell back onto the paved driveway, his mouth slackened as he expelled his last breath. Perhaps from surprise that she hadn't accepted his bribe. Maybe one of his men would have taken the money, and he would've done the same.

However, her survival so far depended on fulfilling the terms of a contract once accepted. In a cutthroat and ruthless business, agreements were binding. There to be honoured and delivered.

Any person on her hit-list was as good as dead. She had never reneged on a contract before. Wouldn't start now. Not for money. Not for anything.

She took the time to observe the area. It was still early for anyone to be out and about in the quiet, neighbourhood of detached houses surrounded by high fences on a cul-de-sac. No lights or movement flickered in any of the nearby windows. Even if someone was out there, they would only see an unidentifiable person in a dark outfit in the rain.

Yahya's mansion stood on a secluded corner. The tall hedges and wall surrounding the house meant no one would see the dead men on the ground. No one would have heard the gunshots. Not with the subsonic ammunition, a suppressor, and the added benefit of the splattering raindrops.

Not seeing anyone else, she squatted and picked the cartridges. She checked the FN's magazine. Fourteen left. Checking was part of her routine for staying alive. She always had to know how many bullets she had available. Even the spares.

Losing count was only an invitation to death.

She pocketed the cold, wet items, unscrewed the suppressor and placed it inside the pocket of her hooded top.

Squatting, she heaved Yahya's body over her shoulder. Then she jogged up the stairs into the already opened front door. The hallway light was on, but she flicked it off. Having studied the blueprint for the house, she knew exactly where to go.

Inside the office, she strode to a Rembrandt painting hung on the wall. She lowered Yahya, glad to be rid of the eighty-five-kilogram deadweight. Searching the side, she found a switch and clicked it. The painting slid along a rail and revealed a safe. Propping Yahya to stand in front of her, she held his head up with her left hand. Once the retinal scanner beeped, she placed his right hand on the palm reader. Another beeping sound and the safe door popped open. An internal white light displayed the content—bundles of cash, passports, and a small black flash drive.

Yahya's body slid to the floor as she reached into the safe. Pushing the bundles of cash aside, she took the flash drive and slipped it into her pocket. It barely seemed enough reason to have a man killed. But the contract had been specific. Kill Yahya and retrieve a flash drive from his safe.

She wasn't here to analyse the reasons why one man should live, or another should die.

Neither did she care about the contents of the flash drive.

Job done. She headed outside, but not to the front entrance.

She strode down the hall to the large kitchen. In the dark, she still made out spotless surfaces and expensive gadgets as she unlocked the side door. Slipping out quietly, she hurried across the garden, staying on the winding, stone path, avoiding the blue, glimmering pool. A small gate stood at the back wall. The men had already disarmed the alarm, so it didn't go off as she shifted the lock and pulled the metal panel open.

Back on the pavement, her gaze swept the area again for signs of exposure, but there were no people or cars in sight, no footsteps to be heard. The rain had slowed to a drizzle.

With a steady pace and ensuring her heart rate was slow, she walked two streets down to where she parked her car, making sure she wasn't followed. Inside it, she pressed the button for the ignition, checked the mirrors and pulled out onto the road. A half-moon sat in the dark sky as she drove the two hours to her apartment in Jokogi. Halfway there, she stopped at a lay-by and changed the fake number plates of the car over before removing her mask and pushing the hood down from her head.

The sky was tinting grey of dawn as she rolled up the drive of her two-level Bauhaus style house and clicked the remote to open the garage door electronically. She drove in and waited for the garage door to close before getting out of the car. The space was large enough for two vehicles and painted white. There was no place for an intruder to hide.

Punching the code for the door, she unlocked it, strode into the house, and made sure the panel shut behind her. She went through each room, checking that none of the intruder alert seals she'd put in place had been dislodged.

The windows were designed to allow sunlight in but remained obscured from the outside as well as being bulletproof. She had invested in solar energy which meant she didn't have to depend on the national grid for steady electricity supply. Once satisfied no one had gotten in or was currently lurking anywhere in the house, she strode into the bedroom.

Pulling the flash drive out of her pocket, she slipped it into a white, opaque plastic pill bottle, stuffed cotton wool around it and sealed it. To anyone else, it looked like an ordinary bottle of painkillers. She strode into the bathroom and put it among the other items in the cabinet above the sink. In there, it looked even more unremarkable.

Perhaps that's what Yahya should have done instead of hiding it inside a high-tech safe. Technologies designed by humans were hackable by other humans. She used gadgets because they made life more comfortable, but she always had a backup.

Stripping down, she stepped into the shower cubicle. Under the warm spray, an image of Yahya slumped on the paving stone returned. His brown eyes seemed filled with accusation.

Her chest tightened, making it difficult to breathe for a few seconds. She turned off the faucet before stepping out. With a white towel slung around her chest, she reached into the discarded black trousers and pulled out her phone. Leaning on the counter, she drew in a long breath and typed out a short, encrypted note.

*Need to confess.*

The constriction in her chest eased when she pressed the send button. She tossed the phone on the counter and went about tidying up. She picked the clothes she'd taken off and walked across to the laundry room. Then she loaded the machine, continuing the routine that restored her life to normalcy after a kill.

Grabbing a water bottle from the fridge in the kitchen, she returned to the bedroom just as her phone beeped. Her heart rate sped up as she hurried to retrieve the gadget from the bathroom counter. She read the message.

*Arufin. 10 pm.*

Closing her eyes, she exhaled in relief even as a spike of adrenaline rushed through her. She had over twelve hours to kill. Time to catch up on sleep. She wouldn't get much of it tonight if everything went to plan.

**Find out more and sign up for LAP book news:**
www.loveafricapress.com/newsletter